L. B. HOLDING

Planted on Perry Street

A Garden Witch Cozy Mystery: Book One

First published by The Words Coach 2021

First edition

ISBN: 978-1-7355734-0-3

This book was professionally typeset on Reedsy.
Find out more at reedsy.com

Bakes.
Thanks for getting this old ball rolling.

Contents

Acknowledgement

Many thanks to the people who helped me with this first Garden Witch book:

Scott Paul of Great God Pan Publishing, or T S Paul as most witch lovers know him, was my first and most important introduction to the world of witches. Before his death in 2020, Scott gave me permission to mention Agatha Blackmore, the main character in his famous Federal Witch series, and her familiar, Fergus the Unicorn. I like to imagine Scott feasting in Summerland, waiting for the rest of us. Thank you, Scott. You are sorely missed.

Magnolia, of Metamorphic Forest, thank you for helping me with all my questions about present-day witches and witchcraft. Your insight has been invaluable, and I look forward to working with you in the next book.

Elizabeth de Souza, thank you for spending time with me and checking me on my characters. Your help with Maddie's point of view and her parents' possible racial perspectives is so appreciated.

Janet, High Priestess at Elemental Magick, thank you for my initial understandings of modern witchcraft and crystals, of positive intent and common misunderstandings.

Thanks especially to my editor, Melissa Molloy, at Directed Editing, who cheerfully took three passes at this book. I so appreciate your patience and feedback on structuring.

Victoria Cooper, thank you for your cover art, such a perfect depiction of Sedona, and spot-on understanding of this book's concept. And Diamond, my neighborhood's busybody cat, thank you for being Victoria's model for her digital rendering.

Nina Made, my original collaborator, I appreciate your support and ideas along the way. Thank you for understanding.

Frank Yim, my friend and support on all things self-publishing, thank you for everything you do for me.

Sandra Abla and Tracy Britton, thank you for your New York State(s) of Mind.

Chapter 1: Manic Monday

Two things interrupted our argument. First, the tinkle of the cat bells I had strung up on the shop's door. Then the slamming of the door itself, which made both of us jump.

"Customer now, salmon later, Sedona." I moved toward the front of the store. Sedona flicked her tail, arched her back, and hissed. "And hey, spare me the attitude, please." I watched as she took a graceful leap out the open window and disappeared around the ledge. I turned my attention to the front of the shop.

My landlady, Ms. Esther Sena, was weaving her way down the center aisle, whacking things with her beat-up cane. She wore her frayed scarf around her head like an old-world babushka that always made me smile, but today she was obviously in a foul mood. My smile melted and I steeled myself.

"Good morning to you, Ms. Esther!" I said, trying to sound upbeat and sunny even as I cringed when her cane clacked against the pot of my favorite hibiscus. "Is anything wrong? Anything I can get for you?"

Ms. Esther lived just upstairs, on the second floor of our

building. She would probably tell you that she and I were friends. Even though I have a very real (and embarrassing) fear of elderly people, Ms. Esther was one of the most colorful I'd met. So, if friendship means lots of time spent together, then yes, yes. We were friends.

She was in the habit of visiting me here at *The Garden Witch* almost every day, usually having made up something that she "needed", but I knew she just came for the company. I had been in her apartment before, and believe me, she was *not* a plant lover, had no need for extra potting soil, or any of the pretty garden accessories I sell.

Ms. Esther loved my tea, though. In the front of the store the walls were lined with jars filled with dozens of types of tea leaves. I blended them with love and just a bit of magic, depending on how my customers' auras were doing on any given day. After shopping for plants and gardening things, lots of my customers loved sitting down for tea with me and getting a quick leaf reading. Even in the heart of New York City, people love the Village touch.

Greenwich Village, that is. Not the little cozy New England village your imagination might place a witch like me. Not the type of village that might still be all wrapped up in clean white snow this time of year. Hedges and fireplaces and woodsy silence.

No, my Village is snuggled up on the west coast of my favorite island, Manhattan, wrapped in the cacophony of city, with the noise, the dust, and the confusion. All things I happen to love.

Meeting her in the middle of the shop, I reached my hand out to steady Ms. Esther by the elbow.

"Ms. Esther," I said, lowering my face so that she could see me through her glasses. I noticed those gruesome black and gray wiry hairs springing out of her nose again. I smiled. We could take care of them.

"Honey, let me tell you," she started, but I motioned for her to turn around and take her favorite seat at my tea table. "It's like the New York I knew as a kid all over again, Madeline. Next thing you know, people will be dying in the streets again, everybody lookin' outta their windows just watchin' bad things happenin' to good people, not callin' the cops or nothin'." She shooed a tiny fruit fly away with her already waving hand.

I sat down opposite her and rested my chin in my hands.

"What happened? Can I get you a cup? Sounds like you could use a little magic," I said slyly. I stood again and reached for the appropriate tea, a nice chamomile for the nerves. I spooned it into the tea ball and pulled the kettle off of my stove. Ms. Esther doesn't believe in witches, but she believes in my tea, all right.

She nodded yes, then went on. "Somebody broke into my apartment *while I was at bingo! This morning,* mind you! Broad daylight, mind!" She widened her eyes and I opened my mouth in shock.

"Today? Like just now?" I said.

"Not *like* just now, little girl. *Just now.* My drawers were opened, Madeline! Somebody picked through my unmentionables! You heard me. I've been tossed! Like in one of them mafia movies! I can't. I just can't. I stuck my things from the market into the fridge, then scrammed. I just can't go back up there. I called the cops. They sounded like I was just another ditzy old lady who got bored and decided to stir up some trouble down at the station. I don't even know if they're comin'! You know, to the scene of the crime."

I bounced the tea ball in the cup while I watched her. Poor

little old thing. She had lived here in Greenwich Village all her life, and while the city was most certainly safer than it ever had been, she was still suspicious of some imminent crime around every corner. I had listened to countless tales from these puckered lips for years now.

For once, though, this wasn't just another of her diatribes. Somebody had actually walked by my window, snuck into the building and broken into Ms. Esther's apartment, while I was busy singing to my plants and arguing with my cat about her lunch.

"What's missing, Ms. Esther?"

"Well, it's a…well, it's personal." Her eyes darted to the right, then back at me. "I'm thinkin' I should probably keep my trap shut, you know how they tell all the victims on the crime shows."

"Oh, Ms. Esther," I said, reaching over to touch her hand. "You know you can always trust me."

We go way back, Ms. Esther and me. Well, a few years, at least, which is a long time in New York City. That's when I moved to the Village and opened *The Garden Witch*. We're on the first floor of this big old brick building that sits very proudly at the corner of Perry and Hudson Streets. My apartment is on the sixth floor, and after a few free cups of tea and a complimentary house plant, Ms. Esther gave me the go-ahead to take over the rooftop, just above my apartment.

Now, the roof is crowded with trees and potted plants, both magical and regular old house species. Just out from the shop this week, they were all spreading their leaves, enjoying the first wave of spring.

"I didn't know you had bingo in the mornings, Ms. Esther." I sprinkled just a pinch of lavender into her tea and offered it to her. Lavender helps to soothe anxiety. She accepted it with shaky hands and more lip pursing.

"I go to bingo at all hours. You know that," she said, after pulling her lips away from the tea. "Gaa, that's hot! Why ya gotta make it so hot, Maddie?! Anyways, I go down to the St. Joe's 6:00 games. Just after my dinner those nights. Wednesdays, Saturdays. You know that."

I closed my eyes so they wouldn't give me away.

"Then there's the St. Mary's game, Mondays and Thursdays, with the before-lunch crowd, where I was just this morning," she continued. "Really? I play as often as I can. Don't spread it around, but once in a while I even go to the bingo bars. You never know, I keep tellin' em. You never know when you'll hit it big!" She tested the tea again and slurped some into her mouth.

I tried to keep my lip from curling up. I hate mouth noises. "Well," I said, "I'm awfully sorry you're going through all this, Ms. Esther. Do you need me to go down to the station and talk to the boys?" I smiled down at her with mischief in my voice, trying to cheer her up, but she was on a roll now, and while she went off on a new angry tangent, I let my thoughts wander a bit.

I wasn't exactly a regular at the 10th Street Station, but most of the cops could pick me out of a lineup. I might have caused a bit of a stir down there one too many times, trying to help them out, especially when a friend or neighborhood merchant had some sort of trouble. And maybe they tend to be a little taken off guard when I use my magic, although really, my magic is very subtle, very classy.

I just think it's a good idea to keep your finger on the pulse of your community, that's all. I make it a habit to know the local merchants, the mail carriers, the cops, and my neighbors.

And many of them, in turn, know me.

My name, believe it or not, is Madeline Brooklyn Bridges. Crazy, I know, but Mother explained that when she married a man with the last name Bridges, she just had to play with it a little. Had it not been for my father's resistance, she would have strung Tappan Zee and Queensboro into the middle name's mix, and people would think I was even crazier than they do now.

I stirred my tea, wondering if I should stick my nose into the business of those boys in blue one more time. While I always felt the thrill of a new mystery, I had gotten an earful of anger last time. I shuddered, remembering that sergeant's threats about staying out of police business. At least he was gone now. Retired, was what I'd heard.

Just then, I heard Sedona land on the window sill. She swished into the front room, and I felt the impulse to grab her and put her out on the street, but she was too quick for me. Before I could stand up to get her, it was too late.

"So," said Sedona, flicking her tail, "I hear there's a thief on Purry Street? Oh, sorry," she hissed as I scooped her up and out the door, making the little bells ring. "I meant Perry! Thief on Perry!"

Trying to cover up Sedona's little outburst, I coughed loud and long, but it wasn't necessary; Ms. Esther's hearing was pretty well shot, and she was busy slurping her tea, so no harm done.

Go figure, but most humans have a problem grasping the concept of a conversational cat.

Chapter 2: Tea and Sympathy

"So you reported it, then? Is there paperwork to fill out with the police?" I reached out and ran my fingers over her hand. Ms. Esther's fingers were twisted and gnarled, and blue veins pulsed beneath the surface of the translucent skin.

"Well, of course. I scooted on down there right away. Didn't even touch the scene, well, except for the fridge, like I said," she said. "They made me feel like I was an ant at a picnic over the phone. So I knew I needed some face time with them. But honestly, Maddie. *Those* people." She stirred her tea and took another tentative sip. I watched as she visibly seemed to relax under my tea's soothing spell.

"What did they say?"

"Yada Yada Yada. They're gonna stop by. At some point. They want me to write down everything that's missing in the meantime, then 'keep my eyes open' for suspicious people in the building. But really, Maddie? They treated me like a damn ghost. Like I was a *ghost*, I tell you!" Her bushy eyebrows shot up and anger flared in her rheumy eyes.

"Ah, Ms. Esther, another sip of tea and a deep breath. Come

on, now." I used my soft lullaby voice and the eyebrows went back down. "I'll help you go through your apartment. You shouldn't have to go through this alone. I'll close up the shop for the day. It's okay." I gave her my best benevolent smile.

"Nah. I can handle it."

"I know you don't want to come right out and tell me what's been stolen, but can you tell me if it's valuable? Like, would it be insured?"

She looked at me for a couple of seconds, then scrunched her eyes closed. "Actually, the piece I'm quite sure is missin' might have some monetary value. But it's the thought of it that matters. It's sentimental."

She scratched her nose. "I'm thinkin' I owe it to Harry to tell him about what's missin' before I blab it to everyone else. So maybe I'll finally give in to you and your friend, Whatshername, and do a crazy séance like you've been talkin' about."

Harry was Esther's dead husband. Every once in a while, my best friend, Hannah, stages a séance and invites friends and customers for an evening with the dead. Hannah has a psychic shop, *Seeing is Believing*, right around the corner. She's half witch, half Romani, and the combination works for her.

"Sounds like a plan, Ms. Esther," I said, patting her little bird-like arm. "I'll give Hannah a call and we'll set something up ASAP. You know you're welcome to stay here today if you'd rather not go up there, right?"

"Well, thanks, but I'm up for the challenge now." She wobbled to a stand and caned her way slow but steady down the two steps to my front door. "Thanks as always, Maddie. Your tea does wonders." She gave me a feeble wave, and she was gone. The bells on the door gave a sad little tinkle as it closed behind her.

I busied myself then, but my mind was definitely on Ms. Esther and this awful break-and-enter that had happened right under my nose. I was confused. When I first signed my leases, one for my apartment and one for *The Garden Witch,* I had been careful to put a magical protective ward over the whole building. I love the city, and the city loves me, but hey, it *is* still a city, and I am still a witch, after all. Use your tools, that's what I always say. Protect what you love.

So, with my ward up and around this building, who could have gotten past it to steal something from Ms. Esther?

I went to work in the back corner of the shop where I do all the planting and re-potting, and as usual, my inventory soothed my mind.

"I know, I know," I told my green leafy friends, "I should stay out of it. None of my business. Never trouble trouble 'til trouble troubles you. Blah, blah, blah." I gave a firm tamp down on the soil around my new Gerbera daisy seeds. I always, always, plant seeds in a comfy circle, then place more of them inside that circle in the design of a sigil, sort of my own magical wish.

I closed my eyes and saw Ms. Esther's face. But then her crinkled old features turned into the strong, proud features of my mother, her intense black eyes boring into mine. I felt a hot rush of anger, and I bit my lip. For different reasons, both women's auras in my vision led me to plant my sigil with the word "loyal" in mind. I knew exactly what that word had to do with my mother, but I toyed with reasons that could apply to Ms. Esther.

When I plant a sigil out of seeds, I always try to incorporate a word's individual letters to make the internal design. I figured the circle of seeds could act as the 'O' in 'LOYAL', so I planted the next seeds in the shape of a capital L, then planted three seeds that jutted up and out from the left of the L's trunk to make a capital Y, finally connecting the right slash of a capital A. (I dropped the final L, because you should never use letters that are duplicated within your word. Or so they say.)

I peeked at the pot, wondering at the different meanings the word "loyal" could take on. I don't know why, but sometimes the subconscious leads us where logic would never go. Heavens know that Ms. Esther and my mother had nothing in common. Except that they were both problems for me.

I stared at the pot for an intense minute until finally two tears fell from my eyes and landed right smack in the middle of the sigil. Perfect placement. Without this light touch of sigil magic, this business of my visions and the tears on the sigil, I would just be another Master Gardener. And Master Gardeners, let me tell you, are a dime a dozen.

"The answer is up to the universe, I know," I continued in my monologue with my seeds, "but the universe or its goddesses gave me the word. Loyal. So that must mean I need to be a loyal friend. A loyal tenant. I have to work on this case, my lovelies. Even if I don't really want to get involved with our friends at the station. Even if they don't want me butting in again."

These beauties would sprout and fill some lucky person's rooftop or balcony pots. Their blooms would bring happiness, and that's what I consider my purpose in life. I whispered to them all the while I covered them with good soil and gave them a drink of regular old water.

"How beautiful you will be someday soon!" I crooned. "Tall and waving in the breeze off the river, like ballerinas you'll be! Just you wait and see."

And then I sang the Magic Lullaby.

When you awake, my darlings,
We'll dance in beams of sun.
We'll celebrate the gods of light
For now, though, we are done.
So sleep and get you ready
For life that's fresh and new
And till the light, all through this night,
I'll dream and wait for you.

"You sound pawsitively insane, you know." The voice startled me only for an instant, for of course I knew Sedona's voice. I put my hands on my hips and smirked down at her.

"Well, what if I do," I said. "The tourists expect a little crazy, and the neighbors think it's endearing. My crazy, I mean." I smiled and gave her little furry chin a scritch-scratch. "You should know me well enough to understand. Think what you will, my friend, but these seeds need the Magic Lullaby in order to help them grow the way I've spelled them. If you don't like it, make yourself scarce."

"Can't," she said, starting to wind around my ankles.

"Can't, why?"

"Lunchtime."

"Oh, please."

"Lunchtime, and someone in this room promised salmon. A girl never forgets salmon." She almost smiled up at me.

"I'll pick some up later, after I make a quick stop at the station," I promised. "But in return, Sedona, you'll need to promise me to not speak out loud in front of people like you did today, please."

Pointless to try, because even as I talked, she had turned on her little feet and was making a very indignant exit.

I had made myself a cup of tea after Ms. Esther left, just out of curiosity. I had a way with the leaves, and usually they had their way with me, too. The trouble with reading tea leaves for yourself is that you can't smooth things over if it's looking like bad times are coming your way. With customers, see, I always try to give the good news, then maybe a real quiet caution about what to look out for when I see bad stuff coming, and then I end on a real light note, usually romantic for the women. And let's face it, the tea leaf customers? Almost all women.

Anyway, my tea leaves were confusing at best that day. I peered into my cup, with the handle pointing away from me, twelve o'clock. Just to the right of the handle was a most definite dagger, but yes, I suppose if I squinted it could be seen as an ant. And gods knew the dagger and the ant carried way, way, different messages. The dagger usually symbolized impending danger, while the ant just meant the tea drinker was in the midst of a busy, productive time in their life.

I sniffed and moved on. To the right of the dagger was the shape of a tiny unicorn, which is never a good sign; it ultimately means you're about to lose something for good, once and for all. I had a brief sinking thought of Mother but banished it.

I sucked in my breath, looking at the bottom of my cup, where two very distinct keys were crossed. Now, like all things in tea leaf reading, this could mean different things. A key at the bottom of a cup usually means a robbery, which was no news at this point. But oh, crossed keys! Crossed keys mean the possibility of romance, fresh and new.

I've been out of college for more than a decade. I'm still

single, and just lately have been starting to think maybe I'd like to be *not* single for the rest of my life. I like to think that my love is being well spent on my cherished plants, my friends, and my cat, but I do hold on to the hope that one day, one magical day, the heavens will part, and the gods will provide me with someone who proves to be patient and funny. Someone who's accepting of my quirky perspectives on life. Someone who will truly love me. Maybe even someone who could cook.

I sighed and kept reading. The last significant image I could make out was what looked like a hammer. Here again, a hammer can mean really good things or really awful things, depending on where it is inside your cup. Today, I was the big winner. My hammer was stationed solidly in the middle of the cup, a symbol for determination and driving ambition, for fixing what's wrong and helping justice to win out over all.

Of all the symbols in my cup, this was the one I held in my heart, because I knew this was the one I could at least try to control. I would fix what was going on in my beloved apartment building, and I would also face my problems with my mother. I would be relentless, and magic would be working with me.

Mother was a problem I had to go alone, but with Ms. Esther's robbery, I could use a little help from the NYPD. I shook off the lingering memory of that last scene at the station and stood with what I hoped looked like determination.

Chapter 3: At First Sight

February in New York is usually a bracing twenty-eight days, and every one of those days, I take my big old green Sharpie and cross it off my Garden Witch calendar. But lately the weather had kicked us all around, up to 70 degrees one day, blizzard the next, then three days like it was the middle of May. I was all about environmental concerns, but it was hard to complain about those warm days.

This was one of those days. Confused robins had started up on their nests again after having to hide away from the snows of last week. The sky above the buildings was crystal clear, except for the white scars left from the jets. People were hurrying along with packages from the delis and some people carried flowers, so beautiful and welcome at the end of a winter. Dog walkers were taking up the sidewalk, and the sweet smell of tobacco drifted around, enough to remind me I used to smoke but not enough to make me want to start up again.

The NYPD in the Village is right down the street and around the corner from my shop, smack in the middle of 10th Street. I'd been there lots of times, mostly out of morbid curiosity. Call me crazy. (Most people do.) I just love to people watch.

Back before I got yelled at, that last time, I used to just show up at the station and hang out, listening to people's stories, watching how the police handled them.

While I was at it, I'd watch the cops themselves, and some of them? Well, let's just say that if they put out a calendar like the firemen do, I'd buy one.

Like I've said, many of the officers recognize me. And while I might have stuck my nose a little too far into their business for their liking, they also know I'm a merchant in the community, active in local events and meetings, and I've never broken a law. Plus, it's a free country. I'm allowed to visit my police station now and again.

I always take a plant with me when I go to the station. You know, as a sort of prize for whoever feeds my curiosity. Today, I carried Venus de Milo, my mysterious Venus flytrap. She was a sweet little thing, standing only a few inches high, but I knew that she'd be ready to sprout her flower later this spring, a flower that would shoot straight out up to eight inches before its white blooms would show themselves.

The mystery of the flytrap, of course, is that it digests insects. Imagine that, a carnivorous plant! Venus' species name is *muscipula,* which means "mousetrap" in Latin. Fascinating stuff, for a plant nerd like me.

I was quite sure there were lots of insects to be had on the windowsills of the station, city or no city. My little Venus, given time to adjust to a much, much louder world than where she was raised, would do just fine.

Surprisingly, the place was almost empty. There was a dingy little waiting room area right inside, with the main desk sitting in the middle of it like a giant toadstool at water's edge. Matter of fact, the police officer who sat behind the desk kind of resembled a toad, when I stopped and really inspected him.

He peered out at me from behind very dirty wire-rimmed glasses, his face all red and puffy. He obviously was in dire need of a good quart of water. A couple of mothers-in-law at home would help, too. Not real mothers-in-law, of course. It's just the name some people have given them, since they seem to live forever. Also known as the snake plant, the mother-in-law gives off more oxygen at night than most plants do, which might help this poor guy. Even his fingers looked swollen, like hotdogs that had been on the grill too long.

"Yes?" he said, and you could tell it was quite the effort, just to say that much.

I smiled up at him and cleared my throat. "Good morning, Officer! I'm Maddie Bridges. I own *The Garden Witch* just around the corner, up on Perry? How are you today?"

"I've been better. I've been worse. How can we help you, ma'am?" He looked tired, so tired I wanted to just put the smallest of rest spells on him, let him close his eyes for a couple hours. Being a witch comes with tremendous responsibilities, though, and even when we just want to help someone, we have to weigh the possible outcomes and what would really be the right thing to do in any given situation. One wouldn't really be helping this cop, for instance, just by giving him a nap. The man needed to take supplements and drink lots of water and cut down on his salt. Anyone could tell him that.

"A little whiff of Valerian, or even a cup of tea with Valerian root in it right before sleep would work wonders, too. Or just plain old melatonin, of course," I said out loud.

"Excuse me?" The officer leaned over his desk and pushed his glasses up onto his nose.

"Oh, sorry. Sometimes I just think out loud. I was thinking

that if you took melatonin? You can get it just about anywhere. It would help you with your insomnia. Or you could pour tea over dried Valerian root. It's a sleep aid."

While he gaped at me with an unabashed open mouth, I put my flytrap on his desk and started rummaging around in my giant carpetbag. My bag, one of my favorite possessions, was literally made from carpet I'd bought at a remnant sale. I have a friend who owns the *Seamingly Impossible* shop just a bit uptown. Sherry can sew anything. And she loves a challenge. Ah, the magic of the city.

My bag is so big that I could carry my toaster, my teapot, Sedona, and a week's worth of food for her, all at once. I don't carry those things, of course. I carry all kinds of remedies and foodstuffs around with me, though. You never know who you'll run into, or who might need a little help. So now I was pawing through the bag looking for some spare melatonin for Officer—

"What did you say your name was, Officer…" I looked at his chest and read, "McCartney? McCartney like Paul? Wow!"

"Actually, no, ma'am." He gave me a disgruntled look and rubbed one of his eyes underneath the spectacle. "It's McCar*tony*. Everybody reads it wrong the first time. And uh, Miss Bridge, did you say?"

"Bridges. Madeline Brooklyn Bridges."

He closed both eyes. "Ah, Miss Bridges. There's someone behind you now. Can you just tell me what you're here for?"

I stopped my pawing. Turning around, I saw a little old lady, tiny and kind of brittle looking. Her back was curved at almost a perfect right angle. Unless she wrenched her little neck, her eyes would stare straight down at the ground.

"I'm sorry. Maybe you'd like to go ahead of me?" I stooped

way down and smiled first up at her, then at Officer McCartony. "I'm looking for something and could find it more easily if I just took my time and sat down, anyway." They both unglued their stares from me as I grabbed my plant to get out of the way.

After plunking myself down on one of the rather shabby vinyl chairs along the wall of the station, I proceeded to take things out of the carpetbag.

A bag of dried liver for dogs who made eye contact with me on the street, a handful of pigeon feathers that I thought might amuse Sedona, the umbrella that had broken a few days ago but I thought for sure I could fix when I got home, the jigsaw puzzle I'd bought on a whim for myself (scene of a New England coastline…it's the Witch in me, I suppose), the library book I still hadn't cracked open (ironically entitled *The Library Book*), my carabiner that held apartment keys to all of my friends' homes, a deck of cards, a plastic silly putty egg, a bottle of water, the little netted bag of gold-covered chocolate coins I'd found for Theo, a boy who lived in my building and whom I was quite sure didn't get enough candy for somebody his age.

Ah, so many things in our lives. I'd have to take the time to clean out this old bag someday soon. Meanwhile, my fingers finally found the container of melatonin, and when I shook it, there was a satisfying click of more than one capsule in there. I collected the other things and tossed them all back into the bag. I stood up and took my place behind the little old lady, who by this time was fluttering her little bird hands around and tittering away to an even more exhausted-looking Officer McCartony.

"I'm telling you," she was warbling away, "*those men* have

been working on the same porch stairs for weeks now. *Weeks,* I tell you. *And* they should be done by now. *I* think they're just taking their good old time, so they can collect more pay. *That's* what I think.

"And my *landlady* is nowhere to be found. I've knocked on her door, and *nothing*. Won't answer her phone, no matter how many times I call. I think something's *happened* to her, that's what I think. I think she might even be *dead*." That last word was in a stage whisper. "It's been all I could do to not come down here sooner. But the *weather*!" She took this moment to clutch her little fist to her chest in a dramatic pose while closing her eyes in a flutter. "Well, I just can't bear the cold like I used to." She let her body sink down to its original alarming angle and stared down at the floorboards.

"Yes ma'am," Officer McCartony droned. "Do you mail your rent to her, Mrs., I'm sorry, is it Pederson? Or do you just take it to her in person? We need an actual address, see."

"It's *Peterson*. Rita Peterson. And I *take* it to her, of course. Save a stamp, save money! But I have her address. I wrote it down." Here she reached into her bag, and I peered over her shoulder to look inside. I was a little satisfied to see that she looked just as disorganized as I was, only her bag was so much smaller that she could barely fit one of her little claws in there. She finally pulled out a red plastic wallet and messed around with the billfold part of it before producing a slip of paper with an address on it. Officer McCartony plucked it from her.

"This is her address? Or yours?"

"We live in the same building," she said. "So yes is the answer." She tittered a little at her own joke. When McCartony just stared at her, she straightened a bit and said, "Except for the apartment number, of course. That's her apartment, all right."

"We'll look her up today, Mrs. Peterson. Thank you for this." He smiled. Or tried to smile.

"You'll tell her I came down in person? Because I'm concerned about those men wasting time and her money on those porch stairs?"

"Sure thing, Mrs. Peterson. Thank you again, and you have yourself a nice day, all right?" He cast a desperate glance at the clock on the wall, then turned his attention to me. "And now, we have someone standing behind you, ma'am."

Mrs. Peterson turned to notice me again, and then noticed my Venus fly-trap.

"What in the world do you have there?" she asked.

"This is a Venus flytrap!" I said. "I brought it as a gift to our police officers who work so hard for all of us." I sent an ingratiating smile McCartony's way and stepped up to his desk again.

"Oh!" Mrs. Peterson said, "You're my neighbor, the garden lady!" She gave me a little wisp of a smile and I noticed, recognized, her perfectly white teeth. Must be fake, I thought.

I'm one of those people who notices everybody's teeth, first thing. I don't know why, but my eyes go there right off the bat.

"That's me, Mrs., uh, Peterson! I own *The Garden Witch*. You've been in my shop before, of course! I remember your face now!" It was only polite, that little white lie. Teeth or no, the thing I really remember, is that she's completely bent over at the waist. Like, boomerang bent, if you can picture it.

"Yes, I've bought several things there. It's a comfy shop. My friends all like it when they come to New York to visit me. You even have a neighbor in your building who's in my Women's Club, I think! Esther. Esther Sena."

I stopped at the name and wondered at the world of coincidence. "Well, Esther Sena is a friend of mine, and actually one of the reasons I'm here today." I put the plant and the melatonin up on McCartony's desk.

"I hope Esther isn't in any trouble?" Mrs. Peterson said, her hands both up in the air. "She seemed well last month at our meeting."

"Oh, she's fine, she's just got some apartment problems of her own. No worries," I said. I watched Mrs. Peterson totter toward the door, then I turned back to McCartony and nudged Venus and the melatonin toward him. "All kinds of presents for you today, sir!"

"Um, I'm not allowed to accept bri…I mean gifts, ma'am." He gently pushed the plant back toward me to make a point. "But how can I help you?" He picked up the bottle of melatonin and squinted at its label.

"I'm just a curious neighbor," I said, dropping my voice into a conspiratorial whisper. You couldn't be too careful. "Curious, that is, and concerned. Mrs. Esther Sena, I call her Ms. Esther because I was raised to address my elders with respect, was robbed this morning. While she was at bingo, if you can believe it. She lives in my building. So you can imagine. I want to help in any way I can. We live at 107 Perry Street? I'm thinking someone here must be working on her case? Our case, really, when you come to think of it. Me living and working in the same building, that is. We're all like a family on that block, you know. Well, and if not 'family' per se, we at least try to look out for one another. And she's old. Older. Ms. Esther, Mrs. Sena, I mean."

Officer McCartony took his glasses off and squinted at me. Sometimes I tend to ramble, and I guess this was one of those times. He took his time cleaning each lens of his eyeglasses with his uniform. I almost opened my mouth to tell him how bad that was for eyeglasses, using regular clothing like he was doing, but I bit my lip and concentrated on just staying quiet.

"I'll tell you what Miss—"

"Bridges, Maddie Bridges," I said, to help him out.

"Miss Bridges. I'm sure that if your neighbor was robbed and she says she reported it, then we've opened a case, and someone is working on it. If what you're looking for is a progress report of some kind, then I'd suggest you not hold your breath. Someone will contact your neighbor directly, since *she* is the victim of the crime. I'm sure you understand." He replaced his glasses and then yawned, one of those big dog yawns that goes on for a really long time, and he didn't even cover it up. I got a good look at all his fillings. I shuddered involuntarily.

"Yes, of course," I said, reaching for my Venus reluctantly, "but I'm sure *you* understand that since I run my business out of that same building and I actually *dwell* under that same roof—"

"Yes, ma'am. I'm sure you will take precautions to keep your property safe until and unless we let your neighbor know we've caught our perp. Lock and key, right?" He leaned forward then, and I got the definite impression he was through with me and my melatonin when behind him a door opened and in walked one of the most beautiful specimens of human males I have ever seen.

Chapter 4: Caught in a Trap

This perfect man, tall, black, and firm all over, was walking right past me and for the first time in all my life, I was speechless. My mouth had dried up and hung open at what was probably a fairly ugly angle, and my brain was rendered helpless.

I watched him walk, no, saunter, past Officer McCartony's desk, and then I realized that he had a little boy with him, a boy who wore a Spiderman shirt and miniature jeans that were rolled up at the cuff. The boy carried a Superman backpack over one shoulder and sucked on a blue lollipop that was staining his lips. Adorable. Watching him helped me regain my composure. I looked back at the man, then bent down to look right into the boy's eyes.

"Well, hello and who do we have here?" I said, trying my hardest to sound aloof but confident. The boy looked up at me through very dark black lashes and said nothing.

"Are you helping your dad catch some bad guys today?" Still nothing, but he switched the lollipop to the other cheek.

"Oh, ha," said Perfect Person. "He's not my son. This is my

nephew, Julien. We call him JuJu. And no, no bad guys today. Yet." He looked at McCartony and jerked his chin up. "You okay out here for us to take a hotdog break, Stan?"

McCartony looked at his watch and shook his head as if to wake himself up. "Yeah, sure. I thought for sure it had to be dinnertime, though. Shit. Oh, sorry," he said, looking down at the boy. "Excuse my French."

"But there *are* bad guys today, Officer!" I said, scooping up my flytrap. "My building was robbed! And I just—"

"Miss Bridges, we covered this already," interrupted McCartony. "I can tell you, er, at least I think I can tell you, that Officer Denton, here, *has* been assigned to your building's case, and you can be assured he will let no stone go unturned in finding said 'bad guy'. But everyone deserves a lunch, am I right?" His eyebrows were wild and graying, and they were raised up in question. "Go on ahead, Miles." He rolled his eyes at Perfect Mr. Officer Miles Denton as if I wasn't standing right there.

I couldn't help myself. I muttered a quiet spell under my breath, nothing outrageous, just enough to slow time down a bit and sew McCartony's lips shut while I got a word in edgewise. And no, I didn't actually sew his lips shut. His lips were moving, but no words came out of his mouth. He made funny faces as he tried to clear his throat and start again, all in silence. I only had a few seconds to work.

I turned to Officer Perfect Miles Denton. "107 Perry, 107 Perry, 107 Perry. Come for tea," I said in a completely conversational tone, right into Officer Denton's dreamy face. He smiled in recognition, I snapped my fingers, and everything was just exactly where we had been less than a minute ago.

"Right, well, we're off," said Officer Miles Denton, and he

gave me a smile which I immediately memorized. "Nice to meet you, Ms. Bridges."

"Maddie. And thank you. You too! Oh, and you know what?" I kind of inserted myself between them and the way out of the station. "Officer McCartony explained how he couldn't accept a gift from me earlier. Which is completely understandable. I keep trying, but in the end, it always goes this way… I give my "Police" plants to people here at the station. People who aren't police. So I'm wondering if you," and here I leaned down to look into the little boy's eyes again, "would like a Venus flytrap of your very own, to have and to hold, to take care of and feed and water forever and ever?" I thrust my plant forward and let him get a really good look at it.

She was a beauty, my Venus. Her little cupped traps had delicate spiky teeth for catching wayward ants and flies, and her stalk was sturdy and strong. She would live many, many years.

"Oh, wow!" Officer Denton said, and he leaned over to get a better look at Venus. "Wow, what do you think, Buddy?" He looked up with a mischievous smile and said, "My sister will be so pissed at me. Thank you, he'd love it."

I had bent over to offer the plant to the little boy, but wow, that smile of Officer Denton's threw me for a loop. Like, I got lost in the whiteness of it, the clean lines of his perfect teeth, and the way his eyes, so black and deep, crinkled up around their edges.

"Um, Ms. Bridges?" he said, and I saw the lips moving, but the sound was kind of in a vacuum. I licked my lips and stood up straight.

"Sorry. Sometimes I just zone out. Not enough breakfast," and I met his nephew's eye with a look of advice and warning.

"Right, so anyway, this is Venus. And Venus, this is…" I bent down again.

"JuJu!" he said, and he laughed, because of course I should have known that already.

"JuJu, Julien, right! And Venus," I said, looking my lovely flytrap right in the eye, "JuJu here is going to feed you and water you and talk to you and maybe, just maybe, if you get very lucky, he will sing you a song right after the lights have been turned off every night." I looked up at Julien. "What do you say?"

"Say thank you, JuJu," Miles Denton said, and his voice sounded like distant thunder to me.

"Thank you, JuJu," JuJu said, and he reached out for Venus. I placed her gently into his little brown hands and looked up at Miles. "So cute," I whispered to him, and he nodded.

"Here's my secret, Julien," I said, using his full name because I thought he looked like a Julien right now, all somber and full of the weight of sudden responsibility. "If you take a water sprayer and give a house fly a good strong spritz? It'll drop like a fly. Get it? Dropping like flies? Ha!" I threw my head back.

"Then, just scoop him up and put him right here." I showed him Venus' little pocket mouth, which immediately clamped down on my wiggling finger. "And voila! Lunchtime for Venus. You can use tweezers. Just grab them by their wings and put them in here, bottom up. Get it? Bottoms up!"

"Wow," JuJu said, his eyes wide and beautiful. "You know so much!"

"About plants, yes. Because that's what I do. I run the shop on Perry. *The Garden Witch.*"

Officer Denton gave me a dazed look. "107 Perry?"

"107 Perry," I said with a satisfied smile. "Exactly."

Chapter 5: I Got a New Way to Walk

Oh, New York in the springtime, there should be a song. It just seems natural in the spring to develop a little crush on someone, and my someone was the beautiful, smiling, tall and chiseled Officer Miles Denton. Talk about magic!

I strolled home, pausing along the way to smell the flowers at *Carol's Cuttings*. You would think what with me owning a plant shop that I would get my fill at home, but unlike my inventory, Carol's flowers were already cut. The poor things were on their ways toward Death's door, and someone had to take them in to enjoy them until they passed to the other side.

I bought a bouquet almost every time I passed by her sweet-smelling store. Today, it was lilies, the big stargazers that fill an entire home with their fragrance. Yes, stargazers are poisonous to cats, but here's one of the very important benefits of living with a familiar, and not just a common, non-magical, pet. One verbal warning about poisonous plants, and Sedona won't be bothered with them.

I threw in a couple of yellow spider mums to give the bunch a good pop of color.

"Thanks, Carol," I said when I came up for air. Sometimes I just bury my face in these beauties for three or four deep breaths. It helps me focus.

Carol Jenson shows up at our Village Merchant Association meetings, but only once in a blood harvest supermoon. I keep telling her that it's not like she has a corner on the market, for heaven's sakes. Florists in New York are a dime a dozen. To make a shop profitable, you have to put some elbow grease into the social side of the business. Social media, network with other merchants, share leads, you know. Everyone does it. Everyone who's on this side of the success fence, at least.

But secretly, I think Carol's husband is funding her shop. He's some bigshot down on Wall Street and I think he just wants to keep her busy. Well, maybe I haven't been completely secret about that theory. I have a lot of trustworthy friends and we spend a lot of time talking about our neighborhood.

"Anytime, Maddie," she said, peeking around an enormous vase full of roses. "What brings you out of the shop?"

"Oh, I'm just helping the police on a case," I said casually. She made a skeptical face.

"A case?"

"Yup, robbery. Neighbor of mine, poor little thing. They got away with some pretty valuable pieces, I guess."

"Wait." Carol took her gloves off and came around the counter. "You're helping the police on the case? Like how?" She had that one eyebrow up and one eyebrow down now. I pretended not to notice.

"Well, Ms. Esther is my friend. My neighbor. My landlord. Landlady, actually. She lives in my building. I'm just lending a hand in case they need anything. Ms. Esther is old, you know. She forgets things."

"But wait," Carol said with a not really so friendly smile on her lips. "Don't *you* forget things all the time?"

I guess she knows me better than I'd originally thought. Or heard more things about me than I'd originally thought. I shrugged my shoulders. "You know, Carol, I'm just trying to be a good neighbor, that's all. Someday, when *you* need a good neighbor, and I step up to help out any way I can, you'll look back at this and say to yourself, 'Wow, that Maddie Bridges is such a valuable asset to our community.' That's what you'll say." I gave her a little grin to show her I was just funning around, but really, I wasn't. I know she's one of the mean ones.

"Ha, you're so funny," she said to me, and I know she had to force that 'ha' out of her mouth. I paid her in cash, she gave me my change, and we parted ways as quickly as we were both able.

"Hello!" I said happily to a UPS delivery woman who was wheeling her box-laden dolly across the sidewalk. She smiled at me without saying anything, but that's okay. My first real job was at *The Fossil Store*, a shop in Brooklyn that sold all kinds of weird trinkets like snake skeletons and sharks' teeth, and I'll never forget what the owner and my first mentor, Broderick Moore, said to me while I was in training.

"Maddie," said Broderick Moore from *The Fossil Store*, "some of these shoppers might not see one smile in the course of their entire day. Except for yours. You might be the brightest light or, heck, the only light in their whole week. Never assume what other people are going through."

Needless to say, I have Broderick Moore's nuggets of wisdom tucked safely under the tip of my tongue, and I refer to them regularly, which drives a lot of my friends a little crazy. Whatever, his wisdom is worth repeating. And on this particular nugget especially. It's worth it to go out of my way every single day to be the bright spot in other peoples' days. Call it a hobby.

Even while trying to be the light in strangers' days, today my conscious thinking was really all about me. Me with that tall dark and way handsome Miles Denton. And how it would feel right now to be strolling along this busy city street holding his ginormous hand, telling him funny stories so that white, white smile of his would shine down on me. Maybe he would cook me dinner in his apartment someday.

With candlelight. And roses. Mmm, I could smell a roast cooking in his oven even as I walked. Maybe another day we could even help his sister out and take little JuJu to a park or a museum or something. Maybe, late at night, he would roll over and—

My beautiful thoughts were interrupted by bird poop landing on my shoulder. All white and runny and gross, it was all I could do not to gag. I pawed through my bag to find a tissue, but all I could find was a slip of paper with an address on it: 109 Perry Street. Which is weird, because that's right next door to our building.

"Well, this is weird," I said out loud.

"You're telling me," said a beanpole of a man who had almost tripped over my huge bag.

He looked over his shoulder a few times, muttering under his breath as he walked past me. I let him get his sidewalk rage out of his system. I don't take things like this personally, believe me. It would be horribly distracting if I did.

I looked at the writing on the slip of paper that had obviously been ripped from some spiral-bound notebook. The handwriting was tiny and slanted backward, which my friend Hannah would say indicated insecurity. Or just plain old age. It looked downright cryptic. Like my Gamma's, actually.

Gamma was my great-grandmother, who had lived until her 98th birthday party, only to face plant into her birthday cake, dead. Such a shame, but also a really good story to tell new friends if I needed to get a handle on their senses of humor.

Then it dawned on me. That old lady back at the station. I must have accidentally swished her address into my carpetbag after maybe putting Venus on Officer McCartony's desk. Mrs. Peters or something. Peterson. That was it!

You can't get much past me.

I weighed my options and decided this was like kismet; I could use Mrs. Peterson's address as a solid excuse for calling the station. They would be looking for this slip of paper. I would be able to follow up on Ms. Esther's robbery. While I was at it, I could follow up on my future boyfriend.

Chapter 6: Something Fishy

I stopped across the street from my building and looked at it. Sometimes we stop really *seeing* the things that surround us. Same with people we love, I think. But this robbery and my new crush had me reeling with life and curiosity, so I took a moment to really look at my home and my business. My life.

It was a six-story building, red brick, absolutely nothing special, but the shop was, in more ways than one, just charming. My friend, Em, who owns a little art supply shop in the neighborhood called *Paint it Paisley*, hand painted the windows of *The Garden Witch* with all kinds of flowering plants, and the color just spiced up our whole block.

Plants hung outside in good weather, and I had loads of bird feeders and baths that attracted more than just your expected pigeons. My shop was a little oasis in a vibrant city that I adored.

You couldn't see the courtyard from where I was standing, but that, of course, was one of the best parts of 107 Perry Street. I looked up to the top of my building, six floors up, then squinted at my corner apartment's windows. They were dirty from a long dreary winter, covered with dust and splattered with bird poop. Surely Ms. Esther would be getting the window washers here soon for some spring cleaning.

I wouldn't be that squeaky gate, though, especially now. Ms. Esther had enough troubles. I squinted again and saw the tops of some of the potted trees I have up on the roof, and I sent a silent spell of gratitude to Ms. Esther for allowing me to use the courtyard and the rooftop, to landscape and grow any plants I needed for my inventory.

I had garden parties out on the roof for customers and friends all summer long, and sometimes even deep into the fall. I'd invite customers and friends, fellow tenants, people from my merchant group, even a relative, scarce though they may be these days. If we got enough people, we would spill down into the courtyard, dancing under my little Edison lights. And in the winter, we built snowmen, both upstairs and down.

I shook myself out of my happy trance, because unfortunately I still had some unpleasant things to do today, most of which had to do with preparing to see my mother. But first, I had to decide one way or another. Do I take the leap and get involved in Ms. Esther's break and enter? Or do I wait to see what happened, just hoping for the best outcome for all, including maybe a visit from the whitest teeth on a man I'd ever seen?

Or do I compromise and just take a little stroll through Ms. Esther's apartment, keeping my eyes open and my magic handy just in case I could be of some help? Maybe I could just give Ms. Esther's apartment a friendly, superficial snoop to help the decision along.

When it comes down to the core of me, I'm a neb-nose at heart. I decided to be true to myself.

I crossed my fingers. Maybe she was out. If not, I was just a concerned tenant, or rather, friend. Looking out for the victim of a crime.

I took the stairway that was inside the front door from the little lobby, past the mailboxes and umbrella stand. Instead of joining the gym around the corner, I climb stairs. My friend Anthea, who owns *Yoga for You* down on Houston Street, told me that stairs were the best bang for your buck, if you're trying to burn some serious calories, which I am. I climb every chance I get.

Inside the second floor, I walked up the hall to Ms. Esther's place. The carpet up here was crazy dirty, and someone was cooking curry again. I opened my mouth to breath that way, since curry and I don't get along at all.

I knocked first, just in case she was in there. From the looks of her when she left my place, though, I could tell she was shaken up and might be more likely to seek out a friend or just stay out in the springtime weather. After a count to ten, I used my spare key and let myself in.

"Ooo Hoo?!" I called. No answer. I slipped in and closed the door nice and gentle.

"Ms. Esther?" I called again. My goodness, the paper this woman collected. I'd been here a handful of times, mostly to pay my rent or report an apartment issue, and that one time she invited me in to help her pluck those nasty hairs from her chin. Each time the place amazed me.

Newspapers were spread over Ms. Esther's coffee table and her pretty old dining table, and stacks of them were sending up little motes of dust in front of the dirty windows. A card table stood in front of her wingback chair, stacked with mail, magazines, note cards, pens, eyeglasses, and books.

News clippings had fallen from the tables, random stories and obituaries and wedding news.

In the kitchen, the old tin countertops were covered with boxes of cereal and crackers, snacks and cookies. An old heavy crystal bowl was filled with oranges that were long past their prime. The sink was empty, and all the dishes, delicately thin china pieces with ornate designs on them, were lined up nice and neat in the drying rack. A dry paper towel lay in the center of a very clean sink, and beside the sink sat a three-inch naked troll doll with banana yellow hair. I picked it up with two fingers and twirled its hair in wonder.

"What in the world? She's buried in paper, she's a perfectionist about her dishes, and she plays with troll dolls? Crazy, how some people live," I said to myself, and almost jumped out of my boots when I heard an answer.

"You're telling me," Sedona said from the floor. "Some people. Some people make promises, I don't know, of tuna fish or salmon or, hmm, let's just narrow it down to *lunch*, and then poof! They take off to solve the latest neighborhood mystery and those of us with no opposable thumbs are left to trap rodents in the cellar, like commoners."

"Oh, Sedona," I said, leaning over to scratch her ears, but she jerked her head away from me and glared at me with giant green eyes. "I'm sorry, truly," I said. "Let me just finish up here and we'll go down to make you comfortable."

"I'll believe it when I see it," Sedona said, arching her back. "I could tell you stories about this apartment...the comings and goings today, maybe yesterday... but maybe, maybe first I'll just go take a nap, and I can fill you in later. When it's good for me." She turned tail and started sashaying out of the kitchen.

"Wait, wait!" I opened the refrigerator in desperation and

dug around in Ms. Esther's deli drawer, which was heaped with white paper packages. I ripped a couple of them open. "Look, Sedona! Turkey! Shaved, the way you like it! And cheese, baby Swiss, hmm..."

"Swiss cheese smells like butt," Sedona said, and I knew it was coming. "Butt hole, to be exact."

"Yep, I know you aren't a fan. Here," I unwrapped another. "Aha! Sweet maple ham! Here we go!" I tore off pieces of meat and placed them on one of the beautiful dishes from the rack. Sedona won't eat from the floor. When she was finished, she licked her paw and gave me a bored expression.

"I was promised seafood. Something fishy. You know how you get your taste buds all set for something? Nothing else seems to suffice. Thanks for the meat, though. Nap time." She leapt up onto the windowsill, and took to the outside ledge, but stopped to look at me through the window. She blinked, slow and with definite deliberation, then surefootedly made her way around the corner of the building, where she would make a ballerina jump to the solid awning of the shop below, then down to the shop's window ledge, where she would slide under the frame to slumber in peace.

"Brat," I said, but under my breath, because you never knew if she was circling back to hear what you had to say about her. I was used to this kind of nonsense, and I knew Sedona would dish if I sprung for some salmon at the corner store later, so no matter. I wiped down the handle of the fridge and cleaned the little plate before moving on to Ms. Esther's bedroom. Because, you know, fingerprints. This wasn't my first crime scene.

Now, this place. This was definitely not the way Ms. Esther would leave things. Hoarder of paper, yes; collector of all things edible that come in boxes, yes; but this room had the air of someone actually looking for something, not how the owner would leave it. Ms. Esther most certainly hadn't made it home after leaving me. I hoped she wasn't alone now. Maybe she was at another bingo game with a friend. Or sitting on a bench somewhere with a nice take-out lunch.

I scanned the bedroom with my eyes squinted, focused. All of the dresser drawers were pulled out, and one of them was spilling over with underthings. I stepped over to the jewelry box; it was open, with several necklaces draped over it. I leaned down to inspect what looked to me to be real diamonds, but I didn't pick anything up. I might not do this for a living, but as I liked to tell people, I know my way around investigative evidence.

I whistled, looking at the way the stones sparkled, even in this dusty light through dirty windows. "So, this wasn't good enough for you?" I asked the thief under my breath. Other pieces looked valuable, too. Diamond earrings, a ring that looked like a real ruby, a bracelet with little round beads that looked like real somethings.

It was all just too weird. Did he get interrupted? That would help make sense of all these left-behind pieces.

But no. I remembered back to what Ms. Esther had said, that she wanted a séance with my friend, Hannah. Something was missing. Something she valued. Something in particular. Ms. Esther knew more than she was willing to tell the police or me this morning.

I noticed a withered old philodendron in the corner of the room. His leaves were covered in dust, all folded in on themselves, and the soil in his pot was like cement it was so dry. Poor thing. I'd take him home with me, foster him like a little patient, nurse him back to health and give him back to Ms. Esther later.

Clutching the plant, whom I'd already named Phil, I locked up, breathed through my mouth down the curried halls, where I felt a definite cold spot. A ghost, maybe? My friend Hannah says they linger almost everywhere. Just a cool swoosh of a feeling, something wispy in the hall that I couldn't put my finger on. After a second's hesitation, I took the stairs. Fast.

As I walked to the corner grocer for Sedona's salmon, I ran through tonight's dinner possibilities. They say that salmon is brain food. Not the canned kind, the real fish. Something about the fatty acids and Omega 3's in it stimulate cell growth.

Maybe salmon was just what my brain needed to put the pieces of Ms. Esther's robbery all together. Sedona and I could share, and maybe she would spill about her day as a spy in Ms. Esther's apartment.

Chapter 7: Here You Come Again

"PsssPssst!" I closed the shop door quietly, even though I knew the little tinkly bells would have already awoken Princess Sedona. Sedona liked to wake up slowly, preferably on her own, which meant I was most likely in the doghouse anyway. The pssst sound was a little bit of a comfort to her, telling her it was just me.

She came into the kitchen corner, arching her back and yawning.

"So? Time to hiss and make up?" she asked, flicking her tail as she watched me unwrap the salmon and tuna from the store.

"They had all kinds of produce on sale today!" I said, putting my apples and pears into the fruit basket.

"Ah, fascinating," Sedona answered, but her eyes gave her away; I saw them widen and her pupils get teeny when she spied the fish.

"Madam," I said, and with a flourish I placed a little white plate with flaked salmon on the table. She jumped up without a sound and waltzed over to the plate.

"Ah, sweet meowstery of life, at last I've found you," she

murmured as she delicately tasted the fish.

"I'm running up to the apartment with this," I said, scooping Ms. Esther's philodendron out of my carpetbag. Its dirt was almost like rock, and not a flake of it had even spilled out into my bag. "Poor Phil has certainly seen better days. I want him upstairs with us, so I can keep a close eye on him." I looked at him warily. "And so customers don't think he's an example of my inventory. In fact," I said, peering more closely at Phil, "I'm thinking this is the poor little guy I gave Ms. Esther for her birthday last year! You need anything while I'm up there?"

She barely glanced my way. "Marty would be nice. For my next nap, I mean," she answered.

Marty Mouse is a catnip stuffed toy no bigger than a silver dollar. Sedona is a little embarrassed by her addiction to him but sheds her pride in order to sleep with him whenever possible. She'd bat him around for a while for show, but really I think he's more like a child's security blanket. She just likes him snuggled up under her chin while she sleeps.

I smiled at her and nodded, but she wasn't paying attention to me. I ran the whole six flights up to our apartment with Phil and looked around the living room for a place for him to live while healing.

"First, a nice long drink, sir," I said to him in a cheery voice. I doused him in room-temperature water, then showered his leaves with the dish sprayer, nice and gentle. I worked with his dirt, lifting chunks of it to aerate it, then wiped the dust off of each individual leaf. Finally, I cooed to him and sang him a nice lullaby. "You'll need a new pot, of course. Let's tend to that tomorrow. And some food would be good. But for now, just some sunlight and a soak in the drink!"

I carried him to the window, the corner one I'd been

inspecting from the street before. "This window," I said, "will get cleaned soon, and you'll both get a fresh start to the springtime." I put Phil down on the sill and lifted the window open to breathe in the fresh air. The streets below were alive with the usual action: people window shopping and taking pictures, cars and cabs clogging up the intersections and honking at each other. Ah, New York.

When I looked down to the corner across the street where I had been standing earlier, my breath caught in my throat and my heart jumped up, bumping around in my rib cage. There, standing next to Ms. Esther, was Officer Miles Denton! Towering and rippling, smiling down at the little old lady, then shading his eyes to look straight at me! Or maybe he was just checking the building like I had earlier. Either way, this was a moment, here, and I was gulping it down like Phil gulped his water just minutes ago.

I watched them walk across the street toward me, Ms. Esther kind of tugging on Miles' sleeve and talking, waving her little arms around for emphasis. Miles just kept smiling at her and nodding his head. Such a kind man. As they stepped up to the sidewalk, I realized that I was leaning farther and farther out over the window sill to follow their movement, and by the time that little realization hit me, I had bent my body all the way out and over Phil, who finally gave up the ghost and tumbled out the window altogether.

I watched in horror. Like in slow motion, Phil twirled and somersaulted, his poor leaves flapping in the air, some of them even tearing all the way off.

And then it happened. But of course, this would happen. Phil's pot–the nice terra cotta kind I always used, the kind that, after falling six stories could probably kill someone, landed right at Officer Miles Denton's feet. The dirt? Everywhere. And the plant? Well, I'm sure he was hopeless, but that wasn't really my main concern, here.

I think some adrenaline-based magic helped me almost fly down the six flights of stairs and onto the street.

"Oh, gosh! I'm so sorry, guys!" I leaned over to pick up Phil's few gnarled little stems that were still hanging on for dear life, and I gave him a little caress. "Glad he didn't hit you!" I looked up and it was like one of those snapshots, you know the ones. The shots you can run through from your life like an actual slide show? The awkward moments, stunning moments, embarrassing moments, they're all there, in some heinous memory bank just holding your life in suspension so you can play through them, one at a time, at your late-night pity parties?

Well, this was one for the collection.

Miles, beautiful and mountainous, had his arm around Ms. Esther. He was biting the inside of his cheek and looking just plain delicious. But Ms. Esther? She was sucking on her lips the way some elderly people do when they're missing some teeth. The little hairs on her chin, wiry and silver, were catching the spring sun at just the wrong angle, calling attention to themselves. Her brow was furrowed, and as she cast her eyes first at Phil, then to his broken pot, then back to Phil, you could just about see the wheels turning inside her head.

I beat her to the punchline.

"Now, Ms. Esther, this is your plant who's fallen from my window. I got him from your place and was just about to treat him to some R & R. You know, some fertilizer, regular soaks, clean leaves...

"That's my plant!" she screeched, pointing a crooked finger toward what was left of Phil.

"Well, yes, he sure is, Ms. Esther," I said. "Like I said, he seemed a little, well, sickly to me. I was just taking him to—"

"You stole my plant!" she said, her voice still really loud. Ms. Esther grew up in the city. I guess she learned early you had to speak really loud out here if you wanted people to hear you.

"Ms. Esther, I just took him in to help him get better. He's—"

"What were you doing in my apartment? When did you take my plant? What have you done with my—" But she stopped herself here, visibly reining in. "Maybe that plant isn't the only thing that caught your eye in my apartment, young lady?" She wrenched herself away from Officer Denton, who gave her a little pat on her humped back.

"Now, Mrs. Sena," he said.

"Don't you 'now, Mrs. Sena' me, young man!" she shouted. "I want to know what Madeline Bridges has been taking from me, right under my very nose! And you!" She poked him in his beautiful chest and spat up at him, "oughtta wanna know the same thing! You're a cop! Do your job, here!"

I was just dumbstruck. I'm sure my mouth was hanging from its hinges. I've never stolen anything in my whole life. Well, okay, that little magic trick with the cups and the ball, back when I was ten. But I ended up sneaking it back to the magic store a few days after I figured out how to make the ball disappear. Human magic is really so dumb. I figured at the time I was just borrowing, not stealing.

"No, Ms. Esther, wait. Let me explain, please." I reached out and closed my eyes and cast just the teensiest of calming spells on her. When I opened my eyes, her breathing was back to normal and her brow wasn't furrowed anymore. "Let's go inside. Have a cup of tea. I'll tell you and the nice policeman, here." I looked at him and felt my butterfly stomach, just like I was back at that eighth-grade dance again. "You'll have a cup of tea, won't you, um, Officer..."

"Denton. Miles Denton. We met this morning at the station, remember? Venus Flytrap guy with the little boy?"

I smiled vacantly up at him and stuck my dirty hand out to shake. Anything for a chance to touch this man.

"Ah, of course," I said. "I knew I'd seen you somewhere recently. Come in, come in!"

Chapter 8: Two for Tea

I turned and let myself into the shop, which still carried that fishy smell from Sedona's latest meal. I wrinkled my nose and lit the honeysuckle candle on the counter.

I hurried through the basic tea set-up, not bothering to ask them if they had a preference on tea type. Usually I take the time to assess auras, to make sure my visitors get the exact kind of herbal supplement their bodies and souls need, but this was big, and I needed to cut corners.

"This is real pretty, Ms. Bridges," Miles said. He was smelling my Star Gazer lily that I'd bought from Carol earlier. He stood to let his eyes wander over my shelves, and finally those eyes landed back on me. I gave him my best smile.

"Call me Maddie, please. And thank you! We've been here for several years now, Officer. You've never been in the shop before? I would think anything on your, what do you call it, beat? Any shop on your beat would be a place you would stop in and visit. No?" I was busying myself over finding little shortbread cookies that weren't smooshed or broken to serve with the tea.

"Well, you're in our precinct, yes. But you're not on my

'beat,'" he laughed. A really deep down, genuine laugh. "I don't walk the streets with a night stick like in the old movies," he explained, coming back to the front of the store.

His teeth were perfectly straight. Like piano keys. Maybe I've mentioned them.

"Oh, sorry," I said. "What in the world do I know about police work."

"Well, that's probably a good thing," he said. "Means you haven't seen much trouble in the neighborhood."

Now I couldn't exactly lie, not with Ms. Esther already here and listening and knowing full well that I tend to place myself front and center any time one of my friends or fellow neighborhood merchants has the whisper of a crime report.

"Are you new to the station, Officer?" I asked, placing the cups down at the table next to the shortbreads.

You're always safe changing the subject, is what I've found.

"Actually, yes!" he said. He pulled a chair out, wobbling it a little in his giant hand as if testing its ability to hold his weight. Ms. Esther, still in a bit of a spell fog, but I promise you I didn't hurt her, plopped herself down, too, and I took my place, smiling up expectantly at Miles, waiting for him to explain how new he was, where he was from, you know. The obvious.

But he didn't keep talking. This was going to be like pulling teeth.

"Are you new to the force, then? Or just this precinct?" I prodded.

"New to the force, actually," he answered.

"Huh," I said after what I thought was an unhealthy silence. "Sounds mysterious!"

"Speaking of mystery," Ms. Esther said, apparently quite herself again, and starting to pick her way through the shortbread cookies. "You can explain yourself now, please." She popped a cookie into her mouth and chewed with her mouth open, making smacky sounds. As usual, her mouth noises made me want to jump out of my skin.

"Oh, Phil!" I exclaimed, jumping up.

"Phil?" Ms. Esther said. "Who on earth is Phil?"

"Phil is the name I gave your poor plant today when I was in your apartment, Ms. Esther," I said. I held my hand up to stop her from interrupting. "I'm sorry, I'll admit that I let myself in with my spare key today after I went to the police station. I just wanted to get a feel for the apartment's aura, you know how I do that, Ms. Esther. Do you remember how you told me you trusted me enough to have my own copy of your key? So that if anything went wrong, I could let myself in?"

She nodded, and I looked away from her to avoid seeing the glob of chewed-up cookie resting on her lower lip.

"Well, something *did* go wrong in your apartment, didn't it? Someone broke into your apartment and stole something from you. Something valuable. Something sentimental, but maybe not worth a lot in terms of dollars. Am I right?" I looked back at her and winced at her open-mouth show as she nodded again.

"Okay, well, you know what I do for a living here. I take care of plants, I sell plants, I breed plants," I explained while digging a nice ceramic pot out from under my counter. I filled it halfway with good dirt and gently placed Phil's roots into the pot, then pressed more dirt around his trunk.

"It makes sense, then, doesn't it, that when I saw Phil... um, your philodendron, upstairs, all withered and dusty and sad, I couldn't help myself. I scooped him up and promised him health and happiness. I took him to the grocery store by accident, guess I was distracted, but then I took him up to my apartment, dusted him off, gave him a nice lukewarm shower and a big drink. Then I put him on the windowsill, and I must have nudged him a little too far. That's all." I smiled a reassuring smile at her while showing off Phil's beautiful new home. He just about smiled at them.

Ms. Esther didn't seem convinced. She mumbled under her breath, crunching on my cookies. I leaned down and focused my energies on her and heard it, the tail end of her sentence.

"...then you came back a second time for the plant, ya little *sneak*." Her jowls stopped moving and she glared at me.

She actually thought I broke into her apartment, tossed it, then went back for Phil. This concept was mind-blowing to me, but it was that last phrase, that "little sneak" comment, that snapped me back into the moment, and in a rush of panic, I checked the wall clock.

It was past two o'clock.

"Oh, my gosh!" I said, probably with my outside-on-the-street voice.

They both looked at me, and Ms. Esther held her right hand up to her heart.

"Sorry, sorry, to both of you, but I have to make a dash for it. I have an appointment uptown and have just been so worried about you, Ms. Esther, that I've completely swept the day under the rug."

I was in a bit of a panic, but Ms. Esther's final words were still fresh in my brain, and they stung for more than one reason.

"I will prove to you, Ms. Esther," I said, "that I did not take anything from you, except for Phil, whom I planned on reviving and returning," I said, my hands on my hips. "And furthermore?" They watched me like statues. "Furthermore, I have *never* and will never *be* anything close to resembling a '*little sneak*'!" I did the air quotes just for emphasis as I opened the door.

They both stood, but I didn't even take the time to catch one more close-up of Officer Denton. He helped to usher Ms. Esther out of the store, and I'm not even sure if we spoke again before they left.

The magic of him had already been sucked out of the room.

Chapter 9: Things We Don't Talk About

Speaking of *"little sneak."*

Thoughts of seeing my mother brought an all too familiar creeping dread. I turned my shop's "Closed" sign toward the street and grabbed my carpetbag. As I reached for the doorknob, I saw the caked dirt under my finger nails. It would be noticed, for sure.

I decided to risk being a minute later to the meeting so that I could wash my hands and avoid the dirty fingers judgement. As I worked the soap suds under each nail, I took deep breaths, turned my attention away from Mother, away from Esther, and even away from Officer Miles Denton. Instead, I focused on Dad.

When my father died last year, he left almost everything to me. And when I say almost everything, I mean all of their money, which was lots and lots of money, the title to his car, everything except my childhood home in Scarsdale. Since both of their names were on the deed, my mother, by virtue of having stayed married, legally inherited the house. She had to maintain it and pay the taxes on it, but the house itself was hers.

After the will was disclosed, my mother didn't speak to me for months. She contested the will, which I certainly understood, but when I tried to arrange a meeting with Dad's attorney to discuss it, Mother wouldn't return my calls. Or my texts. Or my emails. I just assumed this whole mess was a huge mistake, that by meeting with the lawyers together, we'd all get to the bottom of it. Meanwhile, though, reaching out to Mother continued to be in vain.

Already wrapped in grief, I was left with no parents at all.

One day while I was walking in the Village, I saw my dad's very closest friend. His name was Archibald Munch, a name that still makes me want to giggle when I say it out loud. I call him Uncle Archie which usually makes his eyes fill up.

Drinking pals, and originally roommates at Yale, they both had moved to New York after graduation. They fished for Striped Bass at the foot of the Statue of Liberty, bowled in the same league, golfed in the Hamptons. I had spent dozens of after-dinner hours listening to the two of them talk about their glory days back in college.

We did the big bear hug thing, that day we ran into each other, and went to the White Horse Tavern for a hamburger. Over beers, Uncle Archie spilled the beans on the whys and wherefores of my dad's decision about changing his will.

Turns out Mother was seeing another man, but she wouldn't consider a divorce because of "how it would look." When Uncle Archie told me that, I snorted with ironic laughter.

Since my mom is black and my dad is white, "how things looked" to the privileged residents of Scarsdale, New York, was exactly what our family had been up against all my life. It most certainly had never mattered to either of them before.

In fact, my mother seemed to actually *enjoy* the way we looked to the white bread Scarsdale types. We were different. She liked it that way. Maybe the whole cheating, divorcing thing was too similar to what other people in the neighborhood were doing, and she just needed to be different, like we had always been?

I wondered if I'd ever know.

"Your dad wanted you to have the world, Miss Madeline," said Uncle Archie that day in the White Horse. "And the closest he could come to that was to give you *his* world when he passed. To Tom Bridges! You got the last word in with that little *sneak* of a wife, man!" He lifted his beer and we toasted to my father's memory, one of many sad toasts that day.

Things would work out, I was sure. At least today we would have an opportunity to be in the same room together.

I wanted the time with her. I wanted to regain some sense of family, and I was ready to compromise, just a little.

Just a little, because my heart broke for my father, who had spent his whole life working to make his girls comfortable, more than comfortable. I wanted to respect his final wishes, while still giving a nod to the woman who had taught me the difference between ginger and ginseng, between rosemary and Rose of Sharon.

Mother wasn't a witch...well, not the kind of witch I was, certainly. But she had taught me everything she knew about gardening, so for that, I was grateful. Surely some kind of compromise just had to be reached.

She had finally relented for some reason, had agreed with her attorney to meet with me, and here I was, running late. The whole Esther situation, plus the bonus Miles Denton daydream had completely derailed me.

The business of the Mother meeting was to get things about the house ironed out once and for all. More importantly, I was planning on focusing on my relationship with my mother throughout the meeting, sending out healing spells and the very best intentions so that we could start to repair what had gotten messed up. I'd had a bitter taste on my tongue for almost a year now and had grown tired of it.

It was time for growth, time for forgiveness, time to move forward.

Who knew, though? My mother might not be interested in making nice with me after all; maybe her attorney had found some loophole and she was about to scrape everything back into her till, in which case I would, like this morning's tea leaves had predicted, lose something once and for all. Not just Dad's estate, but my relationship with my mother.

Yes, I had sort of dipped into the inheritance, in a manner of speaking. Since Mother was contesting the will, the actual money wasn't accessible, but with Dad's assets associating with my broke little social security number, I had been able to get my hands on a juicy new credit card right after my lunch with Uncle Archie. Going on the hunch that Mother couldn't win back the entire estate, I knew I could make good on the card once the dust had settled.

Plus, I had sold his Audi.

I thanked his spirit every time I paid my rent without wringing my hands over the whereabouts of my next meal. I thanked him when I helped my friends pay their utility bills, or when I treated them to dinner or an unexpected glass of wine. I thanked him when I picked up some surprise dessert for Ms. Esther, a baklava here, a lady finger there. This promise of a nest egg had also given me the freedom to help a few people who wandered around my neighborhood looking hungry.

Somehow, I had to find a way to make Dad proud of me while still letting him get the last word in with Mother.

Chapter 10: Mother and Child Reunion

I had planned out my spells and set aside just the right combination of crystals to help in restoring my relationship with Mother. The meeting was, of course, uptown, because Mother loved the romance of the train from the Scarsdale station in to the city.

I was betting that she had approved of Dad's choice in lawyers. Snyder and Sons, like so many, split their offices between White Plains and the ritzy end of Manhattan, and Mother would surely always choose to make it a field trip, to travel to the swanky part of the island, somewhere north and east of Central Park.

I had a long and rather convoluted trip ahead of me, that's for sure. Getting from the Village to uptown would be a subway ride for me, but I would have to transfer midtown, then take the Q, which was a little stressful and time consuming. I was already starting to feel like I owed myself a luxurious candlelit bath, a dinner out, and a bottle of wine.

For now, though, I closed the shop, spritzed myself with some zest of lemon, grabbed my carpetbag, and left a light on for Sedona just in case I was late.

The subway was always entertaining for me. For the most part, it was populated with native New Yorkers, since most tourists leaned on the taxies and Uber. People listening to music, sleeping, traveling in their pajamas, reading. Some of them met my eyes, and these were always the ones who would receive my spells of peace and love. The magical part of it was that I would never be completely sure as to whether my spells worked or not. Whatever their outcomes, the spells made me feel better, and sometimes that's just enough to keep me going.

I came up for air at the 42nd Street Station. Times Square is such a brilliant light on our planet, isn't it? Like an ant hill where sugar cubes have just been discovered. Everyone is carrying things, moving along with the pedestrian traffic, stopping only to pick up more sugar to carry.

I loved to people-watch, and this place was better than anywhere I've ever been. People all painted up, wearing crazy clothes, scurrying off to see a show, people gawking up at the buildings and the flashing neon above, only to run into scaffolding or other people because they weren't paying attention. People shoved hotdogs into their mouths, screamed into their phones, cupped their hands against the wind around vapes or cigarettes or joints.

I couldn't get enough of this if I lived here all of Sedona's nine lives.

The hotdog smell was too much to bear, so I grabbed one and greased it up with plenty of ketchup and mustard. Late or not, you have to feed yourself, that's what I say. Feeling rich, and maybe for the last time, I tipped the vendor with a ten and we shared a moment.

I ducked back down to catch my transfer onto the Q and stood by the tracks to wait.

A little girl stood with her mother next to me, and I studied them while I finished my hotdog. The girl was nine, maybe ten, that age when suddenly you realize you might not want to hold hands with your mom anymore. Her lip was out, like she'd just gotten yelled at or had been involved in some kind of unpleasantness.

In her arms, she held a troll doll, of all things. Like the one I'd just seen in Ms. Esther's apartment, this guy was naked and googly-eyed, but instead of being the size of my hand, this one was at least a foot long and his hair was brilliant pink. My eyes wandered from his hair to his eyes, and for a nanosecond, just a flash, I saw a glint of light coming from them.

I blinked, looked up. Probably the weird lighting down here in the station.

But no, it happened again, almost a crazed wink or twinkle. It was the same feeling you get when you're the only one to see a shooting star; you literally don't know if you can believe your eyes.

"Excuse me?" I said, bending forward at the waist so that I could be more on the girl's level. "I'm wondering about your troll? Are trolls a trend again?" I smiled and looked from her eyes to her mother's.

The girl smiled back at me and nodded.

"Does he bring you luck?" I asked, the whisper of conspiracy in my voice.

She opened her mouth, but her mother grabbed her hand, gave it a tug, and shook her head. Her brow was furrowed. She looked like she'd had enough of the world, like she was about to explode. Or break. Probably both.

As her mother yanked her away and down the platform, the little girl looked over her shoulder and nodded again at me. After shaking myself free of the mother's negative energy, I collected myself and sent the best spell I could think of while I kept her gaze.

May the universe enfold you,
Hold you in protective arms
And whatever angst befalls you
You'll be sheltered with this charm.

Weak, I know. But I was never much of a think-on-your-feet kind of spell caster. I shrugged to myself as the girl and her mother stepped into another car of the train, then climbed in myself and found a bar to hold onto.

I liked standing on the subway. Sometimes I'd pretend to be surfing a huge wave. I'd bend my knees on my board with my eyes closed to feel the rush, take my hands off the pole and balance while the train shuddered along its track. I liked the kid in me.

Except when that kid had to face my mother. My angry mother.

And here I was finally, up from the station and standing on the corner of 86th and Lexington, my heart suddenly racing and my bag feeling extra heavy. I whispered a little prayer to the goddess Rhea, for her gentle mother's touch, and the comfort that my human mother might never again be in the position to give me. Then I marched myself past the doorman with a tense smile.

Off the elevator, the smell of leather mixed with some men's cologne hung heavy in the air as I swept open one of the double doors to Snyder and Sons. The receptionist sat like a spider, front and center, and she peeked out from behind an oversized vase full of fake, I mean silk, flowers. I waited for her to say or ask something of me, but realized she had no intention of initiating conversation. I tried to give her a good afternoon kind of smile, even as I felt my positive energy being sucked out of me a mile a minute.

"Hi! Madeline Bridges. I'm a bit late, I'm afraid. I have a 4:00 with Brian Snyder? My mother is Sarah Bridges?"

She looked at me like she was just waking up, her squinting eyes jumping from my gaze back down to her calendar.

"Oh, sure, here you are," she said, like her second cup of espresso had just kicked in. "Whew, Mondays!" She shrugged. "Mrs. Bridges is already here. I can take you back to the conference room and get you all set up. Water? Coffee?" She stood up like she'd been programmed to do so. I found myself desperately wanting to do a reading on this one.

"Tea," I said, realizing her stare was fixed on me. "Hot tea would be wonderful, if you have it?"

She kind of gave me an eyeroll, or maybe it was just my internal settings realigning in preparation of being in the presence of my mother. Either way, I got the feeling from this woman that tea was just a bit more work than she'd signed up for today.

"Sure thing," she said. "Follow me."

Mother was reading, as always. Some of my strongest memories of her involve me trying to get her attention away from the book on her lap and onto me. I usually lost.

She did look up from this book, though.

She was a straight-up kind of woman, my mother. Perfectly straight posture, shoulders high and proud, even when she was just sitting with a book. The book, *The Yellow House,* was a memoir that had gotten all kinds of awards and prizes. Mother made it her mission to read every black writer from every country of the world. She immersed herself in her race, except for that part of her that insisted on living amidst almost exclusively white neighbors, buying from almost exclusively white merchants, schooling her child in almost exclusively white schools.

I hope I don't sound resentful. I had an interesting time growing up, but sometimes I felt like it was all affectation, like maybe she had some kind of chip on her shoulder and just needed to continually make the same point.

I never quite got that point, but I had long ago stopped trying to get her to explain.

Today she wore her beautiful hair, maybe a wig, maybe extensions, in braids that fell well past her shoulders, almost to the middle of her back. Her makeup was meticulous, her lips a warm shade of burnt orange that perfectly matched her ten perfectly manicured fingernails. Her smile, as always, showed her perfectly aligned white teeth, as well as her lack of sincerity.

"Madeline, Darling!" she said as she rose from her chair, her arms open for an embrace.

I went along. "Mother, you're looking beautiful as always."

She gave me a final squeeze and held me back to look at me.

"Oh, wow, I can tell that money is already working wonders for you, Love. Look at this, uh, handbag?" Her eyebrows did a little dance up and down as she silently made fun of my carpetbag. "And the wardrobe!" She took her time assessing my black yoga pants, ripped at the hem, and my beautiful muumuu, all swirls of royal blue and purple and red. "Stunning, as usual!" Her eyes moved away from me and I sighed with relief, knowing Brian Snyder must have just come into the room behind me.

"Brian, Darling!" Mother said, moving around me and starting her Hello Show all over again. I turned, waited for it, shook his hand, and took the chair across the table from Mother. After surfing the subway and running around on the Ms. Esther case all day, I welcomed the chance to just sit.

Brian cozied up to her nicely, and I admired him for it; he could have bypassed the song and dance that she loved so much. But of course, he could continue setting up meetings way out into the future, building on his hourly billings, and the longer our mess took to settle, the more he would reap the rewards.

He was a compact, efficient, white man, dressed and groomed and smelling of deodorant soap. He sat down at the head of the table with no paperwork, not even a pen, and clasped his hands, looking from one of us to the other.

We all watched in silence as the spider receptionist delivered my tea, which was weak, watery. I tried to turn my lifted lip into a gracious smile.

"So?" Brian said, "What's to be done, here?"

I bit my tongue, literally, and waited while breathing deeply and focusing on Calm. Today, I would speak softly while still, hopefully, carrying the proverbial big stick, and Mother would either hear me and walk away with some level of dignity and hope, or anger would plug up her ears and she would dig in her heels about her place in this world.

In which case she would leave here with some hefty bills to pay.

Chapter 11: Mother, Mother

"Here's how I see it, Brian," Mother said, and she stopped long enough to lean across the table and lay her hand over mine. My eyes fell to our hands and I kept my gaze there. "Tom was...angry toward the end of his illness. You know how they get. The terminally ill, you know. Angry at life, angry at the diagnosis, angry at the people who are trying their best to take care of them..." This was where she withdrew her hand from mine, rooted carefully through her Louis Vuitton for a tissue, then dabbed her dry eyes with it.

"I just think he must have snuck down here last minute, before, you know, before it got too bad, and switched up the will to make a point. Shake his fist at me and at the world in general. Surely you agree on some level, Madeline?" She looked at me and actually batted her fake, I mean faux, lashes.

The word she had just used flooded me with hot adrenaline. "You're saying Dad *snuck* down here? On his own? Sure, Mother," I said. I started digging in my bag, while visions of Ms. Esther calling me a little sneak flew past me. I could still hear Uncle Archie's toast to Dad, when he called Mother a little sneak.

It was all just piling on.

"Sure Mother," I repeated, pulling out my copy of Dad's final will from my carpetbag. I flipped to the last page. "Pretty sure it was a breeze for him to get himself dressed after having been in bed for weeks...when was it?" I squinted at the date on the will. "Um, nine days before he died a miserable death. You're saying that it's completely plausible that somehow he managed to get on a train alone, find his way here, talk it out with Brian, and then put his signature on a complete reversal of a will that had been in place most of his adult life." I folded the will slowly and put it back in my bag.

"Ah. I guess that's my cue," Brian interjected. He coughed into his hand, licked his lips. "We had the paperwork all drawn up, Sarah. Tom called and asked me to visit him while you..." he shot a quick glance at Mother, "when you were out doing, um, errands. So really," he looked from me back to Mother, "it was just a matter of a signature on the new will."

We both regarded him for a silent moment or two. "When we originally presented the will to you," he went on after another lip lick, "the situation, as you'll remember, ah, kind of imploded. You both left before I could explain the details of the change in Tom's will. And Tom explicitly instructed us to have you both in the room. Together. When his full intentions were divulged."

"Sounds to me," I said, "like Brian has already heard some of our evil little family secrets, Mother. Let's just spill all of this out onto the table right now. About your new man. Actually, not so new man. Or is it men? Regardless, it obviously wasn't my father who was *sneaking* down here to change his will. Turns out someone else is, in fact, the *sneak*."

I clenched onto my tongue with my teeth then, willing myself to be still and to hold my focus. I was supposed to speak softly, here. And I was obviously messing it all up.

Mother gaped at me, looked in shock at Brian, who was sporting a blotchy kind of blush. Mother stood up and put her manicured hands on her hips. "How *dare* you accuse me of inappropriate behavior while I was married to that darling man! Why, the nerve! Surely you don't believe those ugly words that just came out of your mouth."

I weighed my response, all the while measuring Brian Snyder's part in this family passion play. He was resting quite comfortably now, the blush settling down and his hands still clasped but relaxed on his lap.

"I had lunch with Uncle Archie a while back," I started, then turned to Brian. "He was my father's best friend in school. They did everything together, and when he got sick, Archie tried to spend as much time with Dad as possible. They were like brothers." I blinked back the tears that wanted out.

"Yes, of course," said Brian. "Archie was our witness that day we changed the will. Nice guy."

"So?" Mother said. She had taken her seat again but was perched on the edge of it.

"So he told me about your cheating on Dad. For years," I emphasized to Brian, then turned back to her. "Dad confided in Uncle Archie about everything, Mother."

I watched her, knowing she was going back in time. "Dad loved you," I went on. "According to Uncle Archie, even after the truth was out, even after he threatened to leave you, he ended up holding out hope. Thought maybe you'd get tired, change your mind, and stay with him. And he wanted that to happen. Not because of how things *looked to other people,*

Mother, but because you actually wanted to stay."

I didn't say the other things Uncle Archie had told me. I didn't mention that my father knew there were too many ways for him to lose if they divorced. Bank accounts, money markets, stock. Except for her own little account, they were all under his name only, and when it all came down to it, Dad didn't want to risk losing half of everything to a woman who didn't love or respect him.

"The long and short, Mother?" I leaned across the table and placed my hand on top of hers. "Dad didn't want to mess around in court with you while he was alive. So everywhere his name once was, my name is there now. He transferred the title of his car. For all the stock and the funds that he set up on his own, he just changed the beneficiary from you to me. Maybe he did it that way because he knew all along not to trust you. From what I hear, your steppin' out goes back to my middle school days. True?"

Mother stared at her fingernails, bit her perfect lip. Brian was as still as the magical stones in my pocket. I touched them, prayed to soften my words.

"Here's my proposal," I said. "You're my mother. And while I hate what you did to Dad, hate that you did...*that*...while I did my homework and watched television and wondered why my mom was taking so long to go pick up her *prescriptions*, I don't want to be the one who's responsible for your financial ruin. I don't need that on my conscience. I want you to keep the house, and I want to help you. I'd like to pay your taxes."

She looked up at me as if I were going to continue, as if she expected me to keep talking, but I'd known from the moment this meeting had been scheduled. No matter what else spilled out of this mouth, the tax bit would be my last line.

I just looked back at her, unblinking. The stones and crystals were finally doing their jobs.

Brian cleared his throat. "This is an extremely generous offer, Sarah. There is no legal requirement for Madeline to compromise with you regarding her father's will, even after your having contested it. And here she is, offering you the chance to stay in a home that is completely paid off, in one of America's most affluent neighborhoods. Tax-free."

"*The*. Most. Affluent. Neighborhood," Mother said, tapping her orange fingertips on the cherry wood of the conference table. She glared at me.

She had the nerve to glare at me.

I stood up.

"Or not," I said. "Pretty sure a couple of towns out west have usurped Scarsdale's title, Mother. But your neighborhood is still number three." I pushed in my chair. "The way I see it? I never liked it there. Growing up in Scarsdale wasn't quite the breeze you wanted to think it was. So by all means, you aren't required to accept this offer." I turned my back to them then, and I knew they would both assume I was getting emotional. Instead, I was silently casting a last-ditch spell, moving my lips with my eyes closed.

Accept the gift I offer, and many more to come.
May honesty, humility keep anger ever mum.
And as we turn this corner may each of us reside
In gratitude, abundance, resentment now denied.

I turned around and faced my mother. Her eyes were full. Definitely not spilling over, since she was usually pretty careful not to mess with the makeup, but I could tell she was feeling something.

"You know full well that I would need more than my taxes paid, Madeline," she almost whispered.

"And we'll talk about all that, down the road, Mom." It was weird, calling her that, but I wanted to reach her. "For now, just for today, we need to take baby steps." I had a brief flash of memory, a teenaged me negotiating for a raise in allowance and her trading it for potions I had concocted. Beauty potions, sleep potions, she tried them all and claimed that some of them actually worked. Lately I've been wondering if she used my first love potion on that other man.

Regardless, the point was that Mother never gave me anything unless it was tied to some sort of trade. Gods forgive me, but a very real part of me wanted her to know how that felt.

"But I was his *wife*!" She seemed startled out of a trance, looking to Brian for support and shaking her head. The little beads on her braids clicked delicately together as they swayed. "Brian?"

He regarded us both and took a nice silver pen out of his breast pocket, as if to just busy his hands.

"There is another option, Sarah, if you don't want to accept Madeline's help." He looked up. "You could just sell the house and live your life." He blinked, put the pen down. "A will is a will. I can't change Tom's will. But the fact of the matter is that your daughter is willing to meet you somewhere in the middle of all this to help you stay in your home. She doesn't have to do that. And if that doesn't suit you, or you can't," he coughed, "afford it, you are still able sell the house, and live on the proceeds. I've seen the place. It's a gem. And like you said..." He waved his hands like he was solving everything.

"Scarsdale."

I rested my hand on the back of my chair. She looked like a child who has just been told "No" to ice cream on a hot sunny day.

"We can just wait, let you think about it, Mom. I'd like to mend what's broken here--" I said.

"Broken by you and your father!" she interrupted as she turned toward the door.

"...one crack at a time," I said softly.

I'm not sure she heard me, because at that point I was standing in wonder, watching my beautiful mother stalk out of the room.

Chapter 12: Out of the Frying Pan

That's fine, I told myself. Completely expected, I told myself.

I talk to myself the most when my mother is the topic. This melodramatic swoosh of an exit of hers, so typical when she needs the last word. And now, like a lioness off licking her wounds, my mother needed time and space to figure out how to gracefully accept or decline this first offer of mine. In her mind, as always, people were watching.

I said my polite goodbyes to Brian and his little spider of a receptionist, and we all knew we'd meet again in the near future and that this was just the beginning. I could almost see the dollar signs flashing in Brian's pupils as I shook his hand.

I decided to wander toward Central Park instead of jumping right onto the subway. I needed to catch my breath and clear my head.

She was poison to me, my mother. Add in Ms. Esther's angry accusations, and a break-in at my building that should have been well protected by my magical ward, and the sum of that equation equaled system overload.

I needed the flummox that came from this bizarre and

bountiful city to replace the Mother toxins. Just watching the people on the streets of New York is the antidote to almost any ailment in my life.

I passed Bravo a Cuore, a lovely little Italian restaurant that always looked inviting. I considered stopping in to get a bite to eat, maybe even a glass of wine, but everyone I saw inside was happily paired up, starting their evenings together. I just couldn't.

But I could dream, couldn't I? I could dream of me inside that place, with some handsome man, let's say Officer Miles Denton, who listened to every word that came from my mouth. Someone who asked questions once in a while. Someone who insisted on dessert after every meal. Somebody who would be in my corner, no matter what.

Thinking of Miles made me think of Ms. Esther's stolen whatever it was, and while I wandered down Lexington Avenue, I shook off the last words Ms. Esther had said to me.

No one wants the people they admire to think they're sneaky. The fact that Ms. Esther was old was some excuse, sure, but it still stung, after all I did for her and all the time I spent on her, for her to think I could actually steal something from her apartment, something that had sentimental value to her.

I needed her to know that I was a loyal friend. And while my mind went back to the seeds I had planted earlier, the seeds in the sigil of the word "loyal", I realized that my mother probably was feeling pretty much the same way I was feeling right now.

Except she really *was* a sneak.

I closed my eyes and blew away my feelings of resentment toward both women. Right now, I needed to banish all of these negative emotions. Right now, I needed to take action. I turned back toward the subway.

I needed to find the thief on Perry Street.

I came up to Times Square after my first subway leg to get a cab. No time to wait for my transfer. I said a polite but distant hello to the driver, then started digging in my carpetbag for my phone. While I dug, I watched out my window, where a man walked on his hands and carried a fedora on his feet. Tourists tossed dollar bills into the hat.

I adored this place.

Despite the Mother eruption and the upset it caused in my spirit, I still found myself smiling. The springtime flush was upon the city, and hope was almost palpable. Maybe the cold and the ice storms were really gone this time.

Finally, I found my phone in my carpetbag. Some people? They carry their phones around in their hands all the time, but I just can't get the hang of it. It's still just for phone calls, as far as I'm concerned.

"Hey, you."

"Hannah!" I said, still sort of mystified that when I call people they already know it's me.

"That's me," she said.

Like most of my local friends, Hannah Balauru and I had met through the Village Merchant Association. The small businesses in Manhattan's lower west side stuck together for the most part, because we all shared the same problems, the same weather, some of the same customers, the same love/hate relationship with tourists. But Hannah and I have gotten closer over the years because we also share magic. To a witch, the best of friends tend to be witches.

Lots of fortune tellers and tarot readers have good intentions, but it's rare to find one who actually *sees,* like Hannah sees.

Most have a knack for reading a person's face or clothes or scars, enough to make a reasonably safe statement for their futures, and most of them don't get too far off the truth. Humans believe what they want, for the most part.

Ironically, the general public tends to trust the true seers less than the ones who are just making a living. I think their distrust is, in part, because true seers tend to divulge too much information, and the human brain just shuts down when it takes in more than it can handle. Sometimes those who tell the truth just don't know when to shut up. People end up not hearing. Kind of like cutting off their ears to spite their faces, if you ask me.

Hannah's little space is right down on Bleeker Street. It's cute. New Age music playing softly in the background, comfy sofas, low light. She lives in the little back room there, and her life has spilled out into her shop. Stacks of books are everywhere, magazines lie open on the coffee table, and there's always the smell of baking bread. Or mashed potatoes with butter. Or cinnamon rolls. Whatever the smells, they're usually from candles.

She reads cards and palms, and sometimes she gives people their money back and tells them she knows they're skeptical. She won't read people who are set in their opinion to not believe in what she does. Giving their money back just blows their minds, though, and those are the people who end up coming back, she says.

Hannah and I met at one of our merchant meetings about three years ago, and she says she sensed right away that I had some kind of magic up my sleeve. She asked me if I'd like a glass of wine back at her shop, and who am I to turn that kind of offer down? We ended up drinking a bottle between us, and by the end of the night realized that we had so much in common that our friendship was just written in the stars. Or in the pinot noirs. Either way, we have a lot of fun together.

Seeing is Believing, Hannah's shop, closes for three months a year so that Hannah can go home to Vegas to see her family. She has a space there, too. She says she likes what she does no matter where she does it, but the New York clientele tend to be more interesting. Vegas, according to Hannah, is filled with bad booze, skepticism, and people who assume you're just another trained magician. But family is family, she says.

Hannah just kind of leans into her spirit, for lack of better words to explain what she does. She sits as still as a stone and meditates until someone or something shows up to help her do her job. She just translates. Sometimes she's led to the tarot deck, sometimes she feels the need for tea leaves. Sometimes she knows she needs to actually hold a person's hand to feel what needs to be foretold.

And sometimes, a person who has died will show up and talk to her about her client, which I think is just the coolest thing ever. I've tried to talk her into traveling and speaking to big crowds, but she says it creeps her out, the thought of having all those dead people barking up her tree at once. She likes to stick to the one-at-a-time method.

Lately, though, I've talked her into doing small groups, like ladies' nights out kind of things. Three or four women bring their own adult beverages, and Hannah dresses the part, crystal ball, scarf over her head, the works. But the deal is she'll only invite one person's dead, not one per guest.

"I've been back from Vegas for a full week and still haven't had a wine night with you, Maddie! Let's do it soon. I miss you!"

"Well, you'd think you were some kind of psychic or something, the way you read my mind!" I said.

She chuckled. "Really? You called for a wine date?"

"Well, it's a little more complicated than that."

I told her all about Ms. Esther and how she seemed to think talking to her dead husband would settle her down somehow. I told her I didn't know what actually got stolen but described the scene of the crime to her, and then of course I told her I'd met my future boyfriend down at the station while doing my initial research into the crime.

"Whew!" Hannah said. "What a day you've had already!"

I didn't even bring up the Mother Meeting. That one would just have to simmer for a while.

"Well, I'd be happy to help out, sure," Hannah went on. "I have a reading tonight that's sort of a standing Monday appointment, but tomorrow works for me, if you two can make it. It's starting to stay lighter in the evenings, right? So exciting. But it's easier for me to connect at a séance when it's dark. Let's say eight o'clock?"

"Sold!" I said. "Thanks for doing this for us, Hannah. I'll pay you in plants?"

"Please do," she said. "It's almost time for those pots outside to get planted. And in the meantime, something delicious from *Baker's Dozen* would fit the bill, I think. Oh, and did I mention $200?"

We were both laughing when she hung up. That's Hannah. She never says goodbye.

Chapter 13: Somebody's Watching Me

"And now, for a little outdoor housekeeping!" I'd neglected my shop for the bulk of this day, and I needed to busy my hands so that my brain could slow down. I had putzed around inside for a while, straightening, counting the cash in the register, singing lullabies for the plants. All the usual closing tasks.

It was still light out, but just barely, so I grabbed my sidewalk broom and started sweeping the corner, where the dirt from Phil's fall still lay scattered. Something on the sidewalk made me stop sweeping, something that shone in the city's gathering night lights.

I squatted down to get a better look and reached out to pick up two silver-backed pearl earrings. They weren't the kind for pierced ears, but instead had those little vintage clamps that squeeze the heck out of your earlobes, the kind Gamma used to wear. She used to let me play dress-up with them, which is how I learned that if you want to wear earrings, you need to get your ears pierced.

I rolled the earrings around my palm and rubbed away

the dirt. Delicately mounted and almost definitely real, the earrings glinted up at me.

"Phil," I murmured, "you've got some explaining to do."

I'd have to show them to Ms. Esther, of course. I squinted into the shop to check my broomstick clock that hangs just over the shop's door. The bristles of the broom were pointed at seven, and the stick was straight down at the six. Plenty of time to get up there before worrying about when older people go to bed.

But I hesitated. Truth was that Ms. Esther had hurt my feelings, accusing me of stealing from her. And besides, these earrings could very easily have fallen out of someone's purse as they walked over Phil's sidewalk accident. Or they could have dropped from a pocket. Happens all the time. It's a busy city neighborhood.

I took the earrings inside and rinsed them off, seeing for the first time the tiniest circles of diamonds that ran around the base of each pearl. I whistled under my breath.

"You rang?" Sedona sashayed into the kitchen nook, looping gracefully between my legs.

"Hey, Sedona. Look what I just found." I stooped down so she could get a good look. The earrings were clean now, and still glistened from their rinse.

"Hey, now! These are the real deal, right? So purrty!" She sat down and sniffed them. "Where'd ya find em?"

"Outside. With all the dirt from Ms. Esther's plant. The one that fell out our window today."

"The one you pushed out while ogling that tall, dark and Denton, you mean? While you were conveniently forgetting to fetch my Marty Mouse as you'd promised?"

"Yeah, yeah, whatever." I'd let her down again, but honestly, sometimes I just got tired of apologizing to her. I stood up and scrutinized the earrings.

"Ah, the clever 'whatever' teenager technique of avoiding the conversation." Sedona leapt up to the counter.

"Hey, if you were a human, and you were single, you would have leaned out a window to look at that man, too," I said.

"Hmm. Maybe, maybe not. What are you going to do now?" She started licking her paw and rubbing it behind an ear.

"Well, I'm seeing Ms. Esther tomorrow anyway. I'll show them to her then, when I pick her up for the séance. I'm thinking they might not even be hers, you know? I mean look at them," I shoved them into her face again. "Have you ever seen earrings on Ms. Esther's earlobes? Because I haven't."

"Mmm, I see where you're headed on this one, Madeline," Sedona said, her eyes starting to close. "Why, you're thinking of keeping them, aren't you? What, you need the money or something?"

"Of course not!" I was appalled, but something inside me gave an uncomfortable twinge.

"Always with the money thing," Sedona said after a yawn. "Honestly, I don't know why you don't just give up and move to some quiet little New England village where the rent is low, some little cottage with a hedge. Witches seem to like hedges. Sell your plants and your potions, maybe right out of your home. Boring, but at least you could shuck this whole business with your family's will, ditch the stress of it all. Maybe your mother would even like you again."

I was already moving toward the door, tucking the earrings into the pocket of my apron. "But *I* wouldn't like me, Sedona. And we would hate leaving this city."

"I didn't say 'we', I said 'you'. I'm staying right here, no matter what happens. Where are you going?" Her tail flicked.

"I'm going to show these to Ms. Esther, that's where."

I knew she'd follow me, sliding out the window, up to the awning, along the ledge and into the second-floor window. Her words had made me angry, but as usual, Sedona told it like it was: If I could just make enough, have enough money on my own and let Mother have her own way, so many mental burdens would fall away from me.

But it always came back to Dad and his final wishes. I had to find a way to compromise on both parents' angry desires.

Upstairs, the halls smelled of garlic, which is usually an okay smell with me except for when someone who's riding an elevator with me smells of it from the night before. Just another good reason to take the stairs whenever you can.

I knocked with Ms. Esther's brass knocker. I could hear her television blaring from inside. The little hairs on the back of my neck were starting to rise, a creepy feeling that usually is my magic telling me somebody is watching me. Or following me. I remembered that weird ghost of a feeling from earlier today. Suddenly, the door behind me opened. Just a crack, so it was hard for me to see who was in there.

"Who you looking for?" A man's voice came through the crack in the door, deep and gravelly like he'd been a smoker at some point in his life. I squinted to see if I could get eye contact.

I couldn't, but thought I recognized the thin beaky nose. "I'm just checking in with Ms. Esther. I'm your neighbor, Maddie Bridges. I own *The Garden Witch,* downstairs. I think you've been in there a couple of times?" I gave him a two-handed puppet kind of wave and the door opened a few more inches.

He was a thin man, elderly, but maybe not quite up to Ms.

Esther's age. He wore a thick cardigan that hung loosely on him, and his hands, now holding a fireplace tool, reminded me of the chicken feet you can buy for almost nothing down in Chinatown.

"She know you're coming?" he asked, not exactly brandishing his iron weapon, but definitely showing me he wouldn't be afraid to use it.

"Well, no," I hesitated, wishing Ms. Esther would hurry the heck up. I clacked the door knocker again, louder this time. "But like I said, we're friends…I'd shake your hand, but I'm afraid you'd close that door on it. Ha!" I threw my head back to laugh, but I'm pretty sure he knew I was faking it. Sobering, I tried again. "Sorry, I've sold you plants and things at my shop, but I never caught your name."

"I never threw it at you," he said, but his eyes were starting to smile. "Benson. I'm Lloyd Benson. Nice ring."

I looked down at the onyx ring I always wore on my pinky, the one my dad had given me when I turned sixteen. "Oh! Thank you! Well, pleased to formally meet you, Mr. Benson. Are you, um, were you waiting for someone? Sorry if I knocked too loud."

"Nope. Not waiting. Just checking. Every now and then, I like to take up my post. Saw you through the hole, here." He pointed with his stick finger at the peephole.

"Ah, yes," I said. Then I had a thought. "You wouldn't have been looking out that hole anytime this morning, would you have? She's had what you might call an uninvited visitor today, this morning." I jerked my chin toward Ms. Esther's door.

"Yes, I heard. And while she was at bingo, of all things!?" Lloyd Benson put his chicken fingers up to his throat. He stepped out into the hall and I got a peek into his apartment.

Knickknack heaven, from the looks of the bookshelf just inside the door.

"Well, yes," I said. "She told you she was at bingo?"

"Oh, well I accompany her to several of her bingo games, dear," he said, and he swapped the fire poker to the other hand. "But today I wasn't feeling up to it." He stopped talking and cocked his head, his eyes protruding a bit, and he pointed his sharp skinny nose straight up at the ceiling. He swallowed several times, using his whole head and neck in the process. Lloyd Benson reminded me of one of those African Grey parrots in the videos I watch when I need a distraction.

"Well. Sorry to hear you were ill. You're better now, though?" He didn't look sick to me. Old, yes, but definitely not sick. In fact, he looked healthy enough to be able to handily beat someone over the head with that fire tool of his.

"Ill?" he said. "I wasn't ill, dear. I just wasn't feeling up for bingo, that's all." He touched his fingers to his face. "But no, I don't believe I heard anything unusual this morning, to answer your question. And I didn't spend a great deal of time watching the hall."

"Ah. Well, oh, hey! Look who's here," I said, as Ms. Esther opened her door. "Mr. Benson and I were just saying hello, isn't that nice?" Ms. Esther shrugged and mumbled something as she grudgingly let me in. She didn't seem to have much to say to him, which was odd, seeing as talking is pretty much what she's best at. "Well," I said, glancing back over my shoulder, "it was nice seeing you, Mr. Benson. Have a nice night."

"Lloyd," he said. "Call me Lloyd." He shut his door, but I still felt those little hairs standing on my neck.

I just knew. Lloyd Benson was still there, watching out his peephole.

Chapter 14: Apologize

"Ms. Esther," I said following her into the kitchen, "Are you friends with Mr. Benson?"

She scrunched up her lips and sucked on them. "That's probably too strong a word, 'Friends'. But he's a good enough neighbor, I guess. Watches out that little peephole like he's on a submarine back in the war all over again." She grimaced a little, making the wiry hairs on her upper lip do a dance. "I think he might have a bit of a crush on me, just between us girls." She gave a snort.

"He did seem very attentive, yes," I said. "Does he have a key to your apartment, like I do?" I asked, fearing I knew the answer already. "For, you know, if an emergency should arise? Or anything that you'd need a neighbor for?"

"Oh, sure," she answered. "I got lots of copies made down at the hardware store way, way back. Passed 'em out like popcorn." She gave a laugh when I raised my eyebrows at her.

"But, Ms. Esther, why? It just seems like the more people you give access to, the harder it might be to figure out who's behind it when something goes missing. Like now, for instance. I have a key. And now we know Mr. Benson has a key. Who else did you give a copy to?"

I sat myself down on the top rung of her little stepladder that she uses to reach the high spots in her cabinets.

She looked at me like I had bugs crawling on my face. "You ask too many questions, Madeline. Some of my friends have keys to my apartment. I guess I figure that at least one of you will realize I'm missing from somewhere, Bingo or Bridge Club or Women's Club, if I have a fall in the tub or something, and it'll be a quicker rescue for me. I covered my bases, you could say."

I sighed, but not audibly. She's an old woman who is quite understandably concerned about being alone in the event of an emergency, and I get that. But there just had to be a better way to cover those bases than handing out keys like business cards.

"Like who?" I asked. "Who else has keys?"

"Like friends, okay?"

"Friends like me?"

"Just friends!"

"Did you accuse those friends of stealing this thing you're missing?"

"Well, no." She looked at me sideways and busied her hands with a box of crackers. "But then I didn't catch any of them red-handed, neither."

"Ms. Esther," I said. It was time. I hate confrontation. Any kind of confrontation. This was like a distorted version of the Mother Meeting. But it had to happen. "We need to talk about your accusation earlier. I explained why I was up here in your apartment, and I hope you believe I only have your best interests at heart, but I've got to tell you that you hurt my feelings. Right to the core. I thought you trusted me. You actually think I stole your plant?"

"Well, how am I to know," Ms. Esther mumbled, not meeting my eye.

"Well, for one thing? Look around my shop, maybe? I own hundreds of species of plants, Ms. Esther." I leaned in and put my hand on the crinkled skin of her arm and looked her in the eye. "Why on earth, when I own Venus flytraps and birds-of-paradise and every kind of cactus imaginable would I want to steal a plain old every day very sickly philodendron from a friend of mine? Hm?"

"Well, now that you put it that way..."

"Ms. Esther. I need you to apologize to me. You've hurt my feelings by accusing me of a serious crime. I'm sorry, but you need to say you're sorry."

She looked at me, her bushy eyebrows flinching a little. "Or else what?"

"Or else we can't be friends anymore."

Why was everything so difficult? Why can't people just apologize when they mess up? I'll never understand. She crammed a cracker into her mouth and crunched. I cringed.

"You still want that séance, don't you? You want my friend Hannah to work her magic at a séance and connect you with Harry, don't you?" I couldn't believe I was bribing an old woman just to get an apology.

She stopped, and a couple of crumbs fell to the floor. I noticed movement at the window sill, and saw Sedona, her ears pricked up at the sight of fallen food. Ms. Esther took a deep breath, her enormous bosom rising and falling dramatically. I watched as the chin hairs started to quiver, but I held my silence.

"All right, then," she said. "I am sorry. Mea culpa, if you will. I know you wouldn't steal from me. And yes. Please ask that hippie Hannah girl to set up a time for us."

"Ah, well, I already did that, Ms. Esther. I knew you and I would make up okay. Hannah thinks tomorrow at eight o'clock would work well."

"The *morning* eight o'clock? No way!" Ms. Esther said, slamming the cracker box down. I gave a little jump backward. "That's my crossword puzzle time!"

"No, no, not the morning," I touched her as I stood from the stepladder. "The eight o'clock at *night* kind of eight o'clock. We can meet in the shop and walk together. It'll be an adventure!"

"Yeah, well, we'll see, I guess. I still think it's a bunch of hooey, but I'm willing to give it a shot, just to maybe hear the old guy's voice." She gave me a little bit of a smile. "Now, I don't wanna be rude here, Maddie, but I'm bushed. It's time to sleep this bad day off."

I reached into my apron pocket to fish out the earrings. I held them out to her.

"I'm going, but first I wanted you to see these," I said. "They were in with the dirt where your plant fell from my window. Are they yours?"

She put her eyeballs all the way down to look at them, and I was reminded of how Sedona had sniffed at them. I looked at the window, but my fluffy familiar wasn't there anymore. Probably around the corner.

"Pretty," said Ms. Esther. "Never seen 'em before, but they're pretty. If you like that sort of thing, I mean." She sniffed, and I felt an unexpected lurch inside me. If the earrings didn't belong to Ms. Esther, they were mine to sell, right? Who knows what these babies could bring in to keep me from needing Dad's money?

"But wait," she said as I was trying to make my getaway. "You thought those things were mine? That they were in the dirt? From my pot?"

I nodded and held my breath.

"You're okay, Madeline, you know that?" She smiled up at me. "I really am sorry I thought you were a crook. Shoulda known better. I trust you, kiddo." She patted my arm. Her fingers felt like bird feathers tapping on my skin.

I leaned down and kissed her on the cheek. "Well, that is just about the kindest thing that I've heard in a long time, Ms. Esther. Thanks."

"People come and go so quickly, here," said Sedona as I half skipped my way down the hall. She had stationed herself in the window frame of the second-floor hallway. She jumped down to my feet as I started down the stairs.

"And what in the world are you so happy about, anyway?" she asked. "Last I heard you were treating that poor little old lady like a kid who just got caught drawing on the walls. Let it go."

"You heard all that? Her window was closed!"

"Eh," she said, still trouncing along at my heels, "you might just say I have purr-fect hearing."

"Well, you must have exited the scene before the ending, then. When I showed her the earrings, Ms. Esther realized that I was really honest, after all. She apologized for real, not just while I was forcing her into it. I know that she knows that I'm not the thief on Perry Street."

"Ah," she said. "Progress on one front, that's a good way to wrap up a day." She let a healthy silence grow, then added, "That and a nice chunk of salmon."

Chapter 15: Do You Hear What I Hear?

The next day was just another glorious spring day at work. I puttered with my beauties, spending extra time on the hydrangeas that were poking up through the dirt in my hydroponic case. The case is the size of one of those old VW busses, upended, and I have it in the back corner of the shop all winter.

While I worked, I turned thoughts over as if they were the dirt of spring, in need of breaking up and mixing in and getting ready for seed. While I was sifting through the dirt, I had this flash of insight. Phil's dirt had been completely hard, like stone.

I stopped and smiled. Another good reason to believe that those beautiful earrings couldn't have fallen out of the pot; they had to have been coincidentally dropped after, maybe even before, Phil's fall from my window.

I thought of calling Mother, but I knew what Hannah would say: it's important, going into a séance, to be in a positive, pure state of mind, and I didn't want to chance any kind of conflict beforehand on my part. Any conversation with Mother posed a certain threat of rising anger, even if I went into it with hope like I had now, and that might block old Harry from visiting his beloved wife.

I'd deal with her another day, unless she reached out to me first.

A couple groups of tourists came in, tipsy from lunchtime cocktails. They were typical of their kind, women from Kansas looking for leaf readings and selfies taken with the witch. I played along as I always do; it's what plants the seeds for others, friends of friends, to visit one day.

All day, I kept my spirit light and airy, carrying a chunk of Carnelian in my bra, patting it now and then. Carnelian helps those in danger of losing their tempers and those who have resentment toward another living being. You just can't be too careful, that's what I say.

I closed the shop early to allow time for me to center and prepare my mind for the séance. As a treat, I laid down for a horizontal meditation, but accidentally dozed off. I dreamed, happily, about Officer Miles Denton. He was jogging toward me, straight up Houston Street, carrying a huge bouquet of daisies, maybe from *Carol's Cuttings*, only Carol's shop wasn't really Carol's shop. You know how dreams are.

Anyway, it was a pleasant dream, which made me want daisies next time I visited Carol. I jotted it down on my master to-do. I have loads of to-do lists, and I babysit each of them daily, much as I tend to my plants. Broderick Moore from *The Fossil Store* used to say, "Once it's on a list, it's half-way done," and as always, he was right.

After a cleansing and refreshing bath, I looked at myself in the mirror, straight in the eye like Dad always told me to do with other people. And I saw him in those eyes. Sure, mine were dark brown and the lashes curled up black and thick, while his eyes were so translucently blue that you'd think you could skydive in them, but the spirit inside the eyes themselves! I could see my father, proud and funny and unabashedly silly at times. I smiled at myself, at my dad.

I skipped makeup because it closes the pores, and I tied my jumble of black hair back, admiring my neck. I've always loved my jawline and my neck, but of course kept that to myself. Well, who could I tell that to, anyway? I smirked into the mirror and caught the dimples that came straight from my mother.

It's good to take stock once in a while.

A zesty spray of orange all over my body and I was ready to go. My muumuu for tonight was purple with orange lining, crazy enough to attract the dead while still good for a conversation piece with the living. Always my goal.

Ms. Esther was waiting under the awning at the shop's front door when I got there.

"A date with the dead," she said with a wry crinkle of a smile. "That's what this is. If it works. Which I doubt. But why not?"

I took her by the elbow and walked beside her. "You just leave it all in Hannah's hands, Ms. Esther. She's one of the best I've ever known, and that's saying something." She was tottering so slowly that I realized what a great opportunity this was for us; a turtle's pace through one of the very most famous villages in the world, just at dusk, when the dark pushes aside the day and the magic of the city envelopes you.

Everywhere you look in Greenwich Village, life is teaming with energy and force. It is a joy and a favorite pastime for me to watch the rhythms and patterns we move in, sometimes without even realizing it. The cars, bikes, trucks, and pedestrians are all following the rules of red, green, and yellow, waiting for their signals to move ahead, to get where they're going. Honking, laughing, pointing, yelling, but almost all of us are headed to some point B. It's a fascination for me, kind of a game to guess where everyone's point B is.

The walk to *Seeing is Believing* from our building isn't far, just a few blocks on Perry to Bleeker, then another block down. Hannah's lights were already dim, and I knew she'd probably have the eerie and beautiful tones playing. Isochronic tones help release natural chemicals in the brain, and ultimately encourage people to relax and have a sense of meditative well-being. Hannah plays them all the way up to the point in a séance where we're joining hands.

She was waiting in the darkness for us with her eyes closed. She opened them for us, though, and stood to give me a hug. She pulled the blind on the front door and turned off her Open sign, then turned to face Ms. Esther.

"And you must be Esther?" she asked. Her eyes were warm, but very busy, scanning Ms. Esther's face. She took Ms. Esther's hand in hers and cradled it while she talked. "Maddie tells me you're missing something. Something very important. Sentimental."

"Maybe, maybe not," Ms. Esther said. Great, I thought. She's decided all of a sudden to play the hard-to-get skeptic.

"Ms. Esther," I said. "Hannah needs you to be in an accepting state of mind in order to give Harry the best opportunity to visit. You asked for us to have this séance. So now, we need to open our minds and our hearts and let Hannah do her job."

"Well said, my friend," Hannah said, releasing Ms. Esther's hand. "Welcome to both of you! We have the perfect number for a séance, always divisible by three for the best outcomes," she said. "Make yourselves comfortable at the table, please! I'll be with you as soon as I get the soup and bread."

"Soup and bread?" Ms. Esther exclaimed. "Well, if I'd known we were invited to supper, I wouldn't have gone to all the bother back at home!"

"No, Ms. Esther," I explained. "Hannah wants the spirits to feel welcome. Food helps to make the invitation more genuine. And some spirits still seek out physical nourishment." Hannah came back and placed a steaming bowl of soup in the middle of the round table, and some broken crusts of bread beside it.

"Well, it sure smells delicious," Ms. Esther said, picking her chair and getting herself settled.

"Now, Esther," said Hannah, "Tell me more about your dearly departed husband. Harry is it?" She tucked a blond dreadlock up under her head scarf, then struck a match to light three candles that stood next to the food in front of us, but she never took her eyes off of Ms. Esther. "Have you ever been to a séance to speak with him before this?"

"Oh, heavens, no," Ms. Esther said. "He would call this a bunch of malarkey. But this thing is…this thing that's missing…he gave it to me, so many years ago I've lost track. We were just kids. No money, no kids, just a lot of love, you know?" She nodded her head as if in agreement with herself. "I guess I'm just thinking, maybe, since he was connected to it here in life, he might have a clue as to where it is now. Maybe he'll help us find the crook who took it from my jewel box."

Hannah reached behind her to quiet the isochronic tones. The silence was sudden and dramatic. We could still hear the sounds of the city streets, but they were muted.

"Let's all join hands while we prepare," Hannah said, and we each got one of Ms. Esther's skinny little claw hands. "We all need to ask Harry to come visit us, today," Hannah went on, "and we all need to use the same words. We'll say, 'Our beloved

Harry, we bring you gifts from life into death. Commune with us, Harry, and move among us.'"

"You're kidding," Ms. Esther said, after a bark of laughter.

"Ms. Esther," I said, starting to lose my patience. "You need to open your mind, remember? If you truly want Harry to visit with us, all three of us have to be respectful of Hannah's ability to be a medium and Harry's willingness to come forward. Are you still willing to do what you need to do for that to happen?" I looked at Hannah, who had a worried wrinkle in her forehead.

"Okay, okay. I'll be good. Tell me the words again."

"I'll do better than that," Hannah said, placing a piece of paper in front of Ms. Esther. "I've had them typed up so that people new to the world of séance don't feel intimidated by having to memorize their lines."

I watched the old lady bite her upper lip, as if to hold back another laugh, but then she regained control, took a deep breath and gave Hannah a nod. Ms. Esther squinted a little so that she could read, and Hannah and I closed our eyes.

"Our beloved Harry," we all said at once, "we bring you gifts from life into death. Commune with us, Harry, and move among us."

We waited in the silence for a couple of minutes, then Hannah started the chant again, and we repeated it. After another couple of minutes, Ms. Esther started to squirm in her seat like a six-year old who needs a bathroom, but just as we were starting in on the chant again, there was a loud thump, as if someone was slamming a fist against the back wall.

It sent shivers up my whole body. I always love this part, the grand entrance. Some spirits? They just mosey in through the medium, through Hannah. Some of them talk to her and she translates, and some of them take over her voice, which is chilling. Others are either shy or they have trouble getting all the way through, and we have to devise a "yes/no" kind of communication, just with the knocks. I was hoping Harry would talk in words, but hey, we take what we can get.

"Esther," Hannah said very calmly, "You might want to ask Harry a very easy question, or just tell him you miss him, just a little light introduction so we don't burden him. But first, let me see how he'd like to communicate. Wait until I squeeze your hand to talk with him, hmm?"

Ms. Esther nodded real fast. I could tell she was a little freaked out by the magic that the spiritual realm held. Her eyes darted back and forth from Hannah to me, and when she saw I was watching her, she slammed her eyelids shut.

"Harry? This is Hannah. I'm a psychic and a medium, and I have Esther here, who'd like to speak with you. Can we agree for you to knock once for a no, twice for a yes? At least at first, just to keep it simple?"

We waited for almost a full minute while I held my breath, but then we heard two very loud, very clear thumps on the wall. I looked up and smiled at Hannah.

What a gift.

Chapter 16: I'm Not Missing You at All

Hannah smiled back at me and squeezed my hand. I'm always so relieved and happy for her when things go right like this. We both closed our eyes again and focused.

"Esther," Hannah said in a very soothing voice, "Harry has come here to share a visit. I feel him right beside me. He has his hand on my left shoulder."

Well, of course I had to check, right? But no, I didn't see Harry, or I guess what would be the ghost of Harry, standing between Hannah and me. Too bad you can't train to be a medium; it would truly be the most fascinating of magical skills to own. But alas, I would just have to be happy sharing the experience with a good friend who could bring a spirit into this side of the world.

"Harry is asking how you have been, Esther," Hannah said, her voice a little graveled. "How is your health? Are you still dancing every day? Are you eating well? Treating yourself with respect?"

Ms. Esther shrugged a little and opened her eyes. Her gaze

followed where mine had just been, and she seemed to be looking for some physical evidence of her dead husband's earthly body. Her brow furrowed.

"Dancing? Every day? What are you, crazy?" She squinted into the space between Hannah and me. Hannah made her lips into a shushing position, and I could have told her that wouldn't go over well with Ms. Esther.

"Sometimes, Esther," Hannah whispered, "the spirits aren't entirely sure of all the earthly details they left behind when they passed over. It's okay if Harry has his facts a little skewed on some things. Okay?"

"Oh. Sure, okay," Esther said, placated. "Um. Harry? No, I don't dance every day. But I'm eating fine. Maddie, here, helps with that part. She picks things up for me once in a while and finds treats at the store *you* never would have even dreamed of. Very thoughtful, Maddie." She stopped and looked down at the hand that held Hannah's. I think maybe she got the famous Hannah squeeze, which is sort of like your mom's finger under the table, poking into your leg when you made slurpy sounds with your straw at a restaurant. Or maybe that was just my mother. Either way, Hannah usually let you know if you were disrupting the atmosphere at one of her gatherings.

Spirits are sensitive, apparently.

"Harry is telling me he can't remember ever buying you any kind of edible treat, Esther, though he does remember going out on romantic dates," Hannah said. When our eyes met again, she rolled hers.

"Oh. Well, back in the dark ages, sure. And the treats to eat? From Harry, they were definitely few and far between, that's for sure," Ms. Esther replied. "Harry? Never mind the chit chat. I need to tell you something important." She hazarded a glance at Hannah before closing her eyes again. "Is that okay? Is the small-talk portion of this over with yet?"

"Esther," Hannah said with a little more of an authoritarian tone, "A séance is all about the spirit. Not about us. We'll get to your news soon, I promise. But for now, let's be patient and see how this rolls itself out, hmm?"

We let a silence grow while we regrouped, and I sneaked a peek at Ms. Esther, who was doing that lip-chewing thing again. Poor dear. This had to be frustrating for her, having her dead husband so close and yet so far away.

"Esther," Hannah said finally. "Harry is wondering where you're living these days." She opened her eyes and gave Ms. Esther a warning glance. "He says last he knew you were still in the Village but had moved up north. 'Just this side of Union Square,' are his exact words."

"What?" Ms. Esther hissed. She went on in a stage whisper. "If he's lost his whole memory, this isn't going to work for me anyway. Let's just hang up, for Pete's sake." She made a tsk sound and shrugged again.

"We can do that, if you'd like, but do you want to take a chance on talking to him about your apartment first? We have nothing to lose, I guess, if you're going to give up on him, Esther." Hannah sounded like a school teacher who was dealing with an eight-year old after a playground tussle.

"Okay, sure!" Ms. Esther perked up a bit, straightened her back and cleared her throat. "Harry," she said. "Harry, I need to tell you what's happened at the apartment. The *Perry Street apartment*, just so we're on the same page, here." She kind of sneered at the empty space where Harry was standing.

"Somebody came inside and stole my bracelet that you gave me, Harry, all those long, long, years ago. You know the one.

Simple silver band with little diamonds encrusted along its rims. I wore it to evening bingo at St. Joes, you know. Well, I'll never get over it, I don't think, but I'm thinking, you know how I'm always, always, thinking, Harry, I'm thinking that if the police can't get it back, if it's, you know, gone for good, you could tell me which jewelry store you got it from. And maybe I could at least try to replace it. Or even have somebody make a lookalike, you know." She stopped and chewed on her lips, looking at Hannah then me with suspicious eyes.

"Except for whatshisname, the cop, I haven't told anyone about what was stolen yet--"

But here is where Hannah broke in. "Esther, Harry is confused. He's not communicating in full sentences with me anymore. I'll do my best, but you'll need to sit back and just hear me for a while. I'm sorry," she said, and she sounded very genuine as she clasped Esther's hand.

"Fine," Ms. Esther mumbled.

"I hear Hester," Hannah whispered. "Not Esther, but *Hester.* There's a definite 'H' before the name. I hear the word 'bracelet.'" She waited, listening for a moment, then said, "He's talking with Hester. Because of the bracelet. 'You gave the bracelet back, remember? When it was finally over between us? And so I,'" Hannah said, then stopped and opened one eye and cleared her throat. "When I say I, Esther, I mean Harry, Harry is talking *through* me. I'm just the medium."

Hannah was quiet for a while, then lifted one side of her lip and made a grimacing face. "And so I gave it to my Esther. I'm sorry. She's had it ever since.'"

There was a solid and frightening silence then. The three of us, or I guess I should say the four of us, were mute. I actually held my breath.

"Wait. What's he sayin' here?" Esther finally said, trying to disengage her hands.

"Ms. Esther," I said gently, still clasping on to those boney fingers. "You don't want to break the chain, here, just yet. Hold onto our hands until you hear him out, okay?"

"Hear him out? Hear him out? What in your crazy head do you think is left to say, here, Madeline?" Ms. Esther tried to yank her hand away but still I clung on. "He gave me that bracelet decades ago and I've worn it all this time thinking he bought it for me but now I find out it went to his old girlfriend Hester Diamond *first*? Before me? What else do I need to hear, here? If I could kill you right now, Harry Sena, I would do it with these old hands wrapped around your turkey neck so tight you'd turn blue in the face and croak with your tongue hanging down past your necktie! Do you hear me, Harry? Does he hear me?" She looked with pleading, angry eyes at Hannah, who gave a tentative nod.

"Esther, he's sorry. He understands it's you he's talking to, now. Back then, when he gave you Hester's bracelet, um, your bracelet, he was young, didn't have much money—"

"Poppycock!" Ms. Esther finally wrenched her hand loose from Hannah's and slapped the table. She stood up and wiped her hands against each other as if she were washing them. "He had enough money to buy that bracelet for Hester Diamond, didn't he? I've heard enough of this nonsense," she said. "And now I'm going home. With or without you, Madeline."

I shot Hannah an apologetic smile and stood up to help Ms. Esther out of the room. Hannah blew out her candles and flicked on the lights, her lips still moving. Her eyes were focused on something far away, and her eyelids drooped. You're supposed to thank the visiting spirit after a séance, and bid them to go in peace, but we hadn't exactly had the opportunity for that kind of nicety. Hannah was probably tying up loose ends on her own.

As I held Ms. Esther's elbow and started to make our way out of Hannah's shop, my eye landed on her spider plant that hung in the window. Before the séance, she had been glorious in her nearly four-foot diameter, with masses of babies springing from her. Now the plant was browning noticeably, and not just at her tips. Some of her leaves were entirely tanned and crisp-looking. Not a good sign, when you've been immersed in the spirit world. Plants pick up vibes from all dimensions of our world, as do we. Plants just tend to show the results more than we do.

After awkward good-byes, Ms. Esther and I found ourselves back on the street. Greenwich Village almost never slows down, and tonight was no exception. I smiled at a couple of teenagers on skateboards, sent a friendly nod to a woman I thought I'd seen before, maybe in my shop, and then stopped dead in my tracks when I saw a policeman with his back to us. A tall, dark, policeman whose uniform fit him like a blue suede glove.

Immediately, my mood buoyed.

"Oh, Officer? Officer Denton!" I patted Ms. Esther on the arm and told her, "I'll just be a moment. Wait here," and I took off. I tapped Officer Denton's shoulder, feeling myself starting to almost giggle, when to my horror, the policeman turned around.

Not Miles Denton. Nice looking, and I'm sure he was a very nice man, but he wasn't Officer Miles Denton.

The feeling in that moment was the strangest I've ever felt, other than, you know, when I'm putting a spell on something or if I'm meditating and leaving my body momentarily. It was like a punch in the solar plexus, like my breath had been literally sucked out of me.

Like a little kid who wakes up thinking it's her birthday, but it turns out she's just been dreaming.

Chapter 17: Knock Three Times

I walked with Ms. Esther back to our building, feeling lonely even with her clinging onto my arm. Poor thing, I thought, knowing that her prized possession, now gone forever, wasn't even meant for her in the first place. We were quiet the whole way home. I was thrown off about the whole Officer Denton mistaken identity, not so much because that policeman hadn't been him, but because of my reaction. I hadn't had that rollercoaster feeling in my gut since college.

Ms. Esther's apartment was still in a bit of disarray. I put the one drawer back into the dresser and tucked her underpants back into their drawer. She seemed so angry at Harry and this Hester Diamond person that she had shed all of her fears, though. She just wanted to be alone, she told me. I left her there, but when I closed her front door, I just knew.

That creepy feeling was hitting me front-on, the same one as yesterday, right in this spot. Only now, it was hot on my head, almost like two laser beams burning into the back of my skull.

I stopped and stared at the peephole across from Ms. Esther's door and waved at it.

"Night, Mr. Benson!" I said cheerfully, and was met with

silence, but the hot laser beams definitely went away.

I checked in on my beloved plants, and my heart was in the right place, but my mind was nowhere close. I was dead on my feet, confused with what was happening in my head with this Officer Miles Denton, puzzled about what on Earth could have happened with Ms. Esther's bracelet, and finally, since I tend to be an all-or-nothing kind of woman, I allowed myself that nagging worry about which way my mother was going to turn next.

I took a deep yoga breath and tried to focus on my plants, my lovelies. Water isn't the only important thing plants need and crave. They need lots of carbon dioxide, as well as some good old-fashioned oxygen to breathe. But more than just the basics, plants actually appreciate interaction, whether it be with other plants, humans, or even animals. It doesn't hurt to give them a good solid meal once in a while, or a fertilizer treat.

I find solace from my own troubles just by helping others, so after I tended to my babies' physical needs, I settled down in my little corner chair in the back of the shop and sorted through my memory bank for songs.

My darlings loved a sweet lullaby just after lights out, and while I sang to them I nearly fell asleep myself. No sign of Sedona anywhere, which was odd; usually she's pretty happy to see me if I've been gone for a couple hours. I told each of my plants that I loved them, sang a final verse about mice and Ferris wheels, locked up, and made my way to the elevator.

The stairs might be great exercise, but on this day, enough was enough.

It was time to try to center.

I changed into my comfies, as I call them, just sweats and a gigantic t-shirt that has Fergus, my favorite literary familiar, on the front of it. Fergus is a blue-haired unicorn. I've read every book about Agatha Blackmore, his witch, at least twice, and Fergus makes me laugh. Way more than, say, Sedona does.

I put on a solo saxophone playlist, poured a glass of sauvignon blanc, grabbed my laptop, and sprawled out on the couch. Before I could even log on, Sedona came tiptoeing into the room.

"Home a litter late, aren't you?" she asked, winking at me with one eye. I've often wondered how many hours Sedona spends thinking up newcat puns. "Maybe you've been sifting through old clues in your little mystery and need a new purr-spective?"

I smiled at her and winked back. "A litter later than usual, yes. Sorry." It occurred to me that Sedona had teased me earlier about how she knew things about the goings on in our building yesterday. Things that only a cat might be able to observe without raising human suspicions. During the course of any given day, she slunk from floor to floor, from the rooftop to the ledges where the pigeons roosted, and all around the neighborhood.

"You hungry?" I asked.

"Does a dog pee on a fire hydrant?"

"Indeed. Come on," I said, and we went into the kitchen. I grabbed a can of one of her favorites, a feast of tuna and liver, and spooned it into her little silver dish.

As I freshened her water, I said, "Sedona, about the Ms. Esther robbery..."

"Hmmm," she said. She looked up from her bowl, licked her lips, and returned to her food.

"I'm wondering if you might have seen anything yesterday that was, I don't know, out of place or unusual? If maybe you were anywhere near Ms. Esther's apartment, maybe when it was robbed, or even right after? You know, like you mentioned."

"Hmmm," she said again, and I remembered how she hated it when I talked to her during a meal. I decided to shut up and let her finish. I sipped my wine and hummed along to the music. Grover Washington, Jr. on his sax makes everything feel better.

Finally, Sedona sat in front of her empty dish and proceeded to bathe herself.

"You want to groom yourself in the other room? Talk for a bit?" I asked.

She sighed. "Fine, Maddie. But I'm not sure I have anything *that* significant to tell you." She turned and left the room, her tail at high mast.

"Do you know the guy who lives across the hall from Ms. Esther?" I asked. I watched her plop herself down at the opposite side of the couch. She picked up her left front paw.

"Little guy? Weirdly spaced whiskers?" she said.

"I guess," I said, scratching my head. "To be honest, I don't think I noticed his whiskers. Looks a little like Mr. Rogers?"

"After a really hard day in the neighborhood, maybe, sure," Sedona said. She bent back over her paw and closed her eyes while she licked it. "Kind of creepy, though. Talks to himself." She took the clean paw and raked it over her ear.

"Hm. He was sort of stationed at his peephole, just watching, when I checked in with Ms. Esther last night, and then again tonight when I dropped her off."

"Maybe he likes her," Sedona said, opening her eyes a crack. "Maybe he likes *lots* of ladies."

"Maybe," I said. "But I felt more like he'd just been standing there, waiting behind his door. He had no idea when we'd be getting back. Does that mean he was just standing there? For what, a couple hours?"

"Maybe he's fixated on her. Can't get Ms. Esther out of his mind sort of thing. Love does weird and wonderful things to us, you know, Maddie." Sedona flicked her tail and looked at me with a steady gaze.

"I guess you could have something there," I said. "So you don't really have anything for me in the way of clues? Like you *said* you might. Before I *fed you*." I didn't mean to, but I might have glared at her. She always did this, teasing me with some juicy bit of information just to get food, then totally dissing me.

"Well, not really, no," she said. "I was just about to say that I am all talked out, here. Thanks for sparing a few moments of your day for the likes of me—ow," she added in her haughty, sarcastic voice, and she leaped down from her cushion to saunter out of the room.

She really is a nice cat; we had just been a bit off lately. Like most of us, Sedona likes attention, and I guessed I hadn't been giving her that, given my distractions.

"Either way, I should probably call Hannah and check in with her. She probably has more from Harry than she let on tonight," I said to the empty room.

Hannah was an early-to-bed kind of person, and I wanted to get to her before she turned in for the night. I looked up to my living room wall, where my wise old owl clock ticked. Her tailfeathers acted as the pendulum, her spectacled eyes were at half-mast, moving back and forth with the seconds, and right now her one wing pointed at the nine and the other was straight up at the twelve.

I took the chance. Hannah answered on the first ring, with a little bit of a shake in her voice.

"Hey," I said. "Just wanted to check in with you, tell you thanks again for the séance. Sorry she was kind of a handful."

"She was the least of my problems tonight, Maddie," Hannah said. "Harry was kind of a big deal, though, let me tell you."

"Can you talk?" I jumped at the chance to spend time with her, especially if she had news from Harry. "Too late for that wine date? I have pizza!" My mouth started watering as I talked. When was the last time I ate, I wondered?

"Perfect," Hannah answered, and hung up. Even on the phone, it's like Hannah's still right beside me.

While I waited, I could use the time to center. Hannah being Hannah, she could be here in minutes, or she could very well be here hours from now.

Being a witch has its definite advantages. Meditation mixed with just a pinch of my magic helps me transport my conscience into the gap that exists between the real world and the true world.

I know, that's a lot to swallow.

The real world is where we all are, hustling to work every day, scrubbing our bodies, eating our meals, talking, laughing, worrying. Doing worldly things. Earthly things.

The true world, though, that's a harder thing to describe. Imagine not thinking at all. Just being. That's the world where, if you're a good witch, and most of us are, you are able to revel in your existence, connecting to the universe for hours at a time.

If you have hours at a time.

Which most of us don't, so I take what I can get.

I lit the candles, turned off the lights and music, and cracked my neck and my back, which I do at least once a day just to stay comfortable. I was in a car accident when I was a little girl and still have spinal problems, but that's another story, and it's a long one.

I held my copper nugget in my left hand, having carefully removed it from its home in my underwear drawer, and in the right hand I squeezed my smoky quartz, to help me gain balance, clarity, and a bit of grounding. My smoky quartz helps me sort things out, pulling apart a big problem into tiny bite-sized pieces, somehow making the problem seem much simpler than what it had once been.

I floated there, in the true world, eyes closed, with even breath and just a ghost of a smile on my face, for what seemed like a full night's rest. I lost Ms. Esther's robbery, I lost worries about the Mother Meeting, and I even managed to lose thoughts of Officer Miles Denton. This was life and awareness as it was meant to be. I sighed and let my head fall back onto the back of the couch.

Three loud knocks jolted me back into the world, the world where people steal from and cheat on each other and cats get indignant and police officers are just out of reach.

I looked at my wall clock. Now, the owl's eyes were wide open, and her wings were high over her head.

It was midnight.

The witching hour.

Chapter 18: Up on a Roof

"Hannah! What in the world?" I opened my door wider and let Hannah in. She was shivering from the spring wind and goosebumps dotted her bare arms. She gave me a weak smile.

"What? I said I could come over, I came over. Took a nap first." She looked around and smiled when Sedona walked in. "Hey, Sedona! How's tricks?"

"The only trick I would be able to do right now is see in the dark. But oh, wait," Sedona said, flicking her tail. "It's midnight, and the lights are on. Hmm." She sent a disdainful stare Hannah's way. "I'm thinking midnight, midnight, what goes with midnight…Oh, I've got one! Snack! Let's all help ourselves to a midnight snack, hmm?"

I shrugged, and we followed her into the kitchen.

I crushed some fresh basil and thyme with my mortar and pestle and turned on the oven. "So? What's old Harry been up to? I saw you whispering to him as we were leaving."

Hannah took a hair tie off her wrist and yanked her blond dreadlocks into a messy ponytail. She sat at my kitchen table and looked up at me. "He left me understandably upset. You, know, first time visiting the living and he throws himself under the bus. But there's more, Maddie."

She stood to reach into my freezer and opened the pizza box. "I was getting so many strange things while it was going on, but I wasn't sure how to interpret them. I kept it all to myself, because I didn't want to upset or confuse Esther, but I knew you'd want to hear about it." She bit her lip.

"You mean stranger than her dead husband mistaking her for his old girlfriend? Stranger than finding out the bracelet she's missing used to *be* his old girlfriend's? Poor Ms. Esther," I said, grabbing us two beers from the fridge. Hannah put her hand up and shook her head, so I put hers back. "What else?"

"Well, first of all, I was getting images of other people in my third eye. One of them was a little old lady, not Esther, but I know in my heart it wasn't this Hester woman, either."

"How would you know that?"

"I just do. It's hard to explain." She got up and poured herself a glass of water from my tap. Brave woman.

"This little old lady," she went on, "was stooped over. Like in a yoga tabletop pose. She was maybe older than Esther by a few years. She was standing on some porch or stoop, wagging her finger back and forth. Then I saw her with a cop. Like she was filing some kind of complaint. It was the weirdest thing. I don't know, I got this really strong feeling that she knows either you or Esther. Because I've never seen her before, I'm sure."

"That *is* weird," I said. "Anything else?"

"Yes! When the older lady went out of my head, she was immediately replaced by a troll."

"A troll."

"Yes, a troll. A blue-haired troll. You know, the kind you

played with as a kid. Goofy big eyes, big belly, long hair we used to braid?" She took a sip of water and looked longingly at the oven. "Does it really need to preheat?"

"Nah. Pop it in."

She tossed my ground spices onto the pizza and slid it in.

"Me. Ow." Sedona leaped up onto the kitchen counter. "What's a girl gotta do around this joint to get some vittles?"

"Oh, wow. Sorry, Sedona. You must be starving!" I rolled my eyes at Hannah. This cat was always hungry. I jumped up and got to work on her midnight snack.

"So. A troll. With blue hair. Was in your head at the séance."

"Yes!"

"And you're here to try to figure that out."

"Exactly. Where's your wine." Hannah stuck her head in my fridge and pulled out the bottle. She busied herself with a glass and ice, lots of ice. She always drowns the wine with a full glass of ice.

"Last thing Harry says to me?" Hannah said, taking a sip. "I'll see my Esther soon."

"That's not really that odd, though is it?" I asked. "I mean, spirit world time is way different than ours, right? That could just be wishful thinking." I looked into Hannah's eyes and we gave each other just inkling smiles. "I'm thinking we need a little fresh air, a little candlelight, and a little night magic," I said. "You want to go to the roof?"

"I thought you'd never ask," Hannah said. "But can we wait for pizza first?"

I put Sedona's snack, a pinch of tuna and a couple of treats in a tiny bowl, onto the table and started rummaging through my candle drawer. I have every color candle you can imagine. Every spell I cast needs a different color. Red candles for courage spells, yellow for empowerment, blue for healing and patience spells, purple for ambition, the list goes on. You name it, there's a spell with a candle that can help make it happen.

Tonight, I picked up a slender silver candle and bent down to grab four little muslin bags from under the sink. Before I got to the door, I leaned over, said a few words to my sage plant, and borrowed some of her leaves.

"Come on," I said. I saw Hannah's face, stuffed with pizza, and grabbed a piece for myself. I lifted my lip at her when I felt the edges, still almost frozen. "Hannah--"

But she was already in the living room, ready to go.

"Hey, leave the door open a whisker, please?" Sedona looked up from her bowl. "I'd rather take the stairs than the ledges and awnings tonight? If it's okay that I join you, that is." She licked her lips and the tip of her tail twitched.

"Things are getting stolen around here, Sedona," I said, tweaking a bay leaf from my plant that stays in my kitchen almost all year long. "I know we've had a second-rate time of it lately, you and me, but I'm sorry. Door gets locked. Use the window." I have a window that's in the back of the building, where, in my mind at least, no bad guys could reach from the street. There's a ledge that runs around the building that Sedona uses. But usually, she'd rather not.

She was still staring at me when the door closed behind us.

"She's a cat," I said to Hannah when I caught up with her. She made a sympathy face.

"She's a cat who talks, Maddie. And knows spells. I don't know how much I'd push her, if I were you." Hannah made little huffing sounds as we climbed up the flight of stairs.

"Sounds like you need exercise just like my fat cat," I said.

She knew I was kidding. We kid around a lot.

"What are you collecting up here tonight?" she asked. We had reached the rooftop. The moon and lights from the city made it almost as bright out here as it is in the daytime. My plants all looked healthy, despite the changing temperatures. Old-fashioned rain and sunshine do their share of good, but a little taste of magic now and then really does the trick.

I walked the perimeter of the roof, touching leaves and murmuring greetings and words of adoration to all of them. Herbs, shrubs, baby trees still in their pots, they were all here waiting eagerly for the summer. My perennials were just starting to peek out, looking for their annual friends whom I'd planted inside. All of them, used just the right way, were magical.

"Tonight, my friend?" I said, waving my hands like a gameshow host, "we will be needing several species, all working together. My candle and our good intentions need to come from our hearts, as always, but the earth's gifts will be the catalysts of dreams." I stooped down and plucked up a dried holly leaf that had fallen from my male holly tree. I thanked him as I stood.

Then I walked over to the ash tree that I'm hoping to plant this spring in the courtyard downstairs unless someone buys him. I thanked him first, because his leaf needed to come straight from him, and I hated to think I was hurting him. Gently, I squeezed off a single leaf and thanked him again.

"You know, maybe we won't even give them a chance to buy you," I said, stroking his delicate little trunk. "Maybe we'll just plop you in the ground before anyone even gets a look at you." I smiled, ripped his leaf into bits, and placed the pieces into my apron along with the holly, bay and sage leaves.

Hannah and I sat on two weather-proof mats right in the

middle of the roof. We sat for a minute or two in amicable silence, settling in to the rhythm of the city, the cabs honking at each other, the steady sound of traffic, the occasional shout from the sidewalk. Hannah and I were kindred spirits in many ways. Witches, meditators, well-intentioned souls looking to make our world better. But most importantly, we loved our city, especially our own little homey corner of it, our town within this incredible metropolis. We loved our Village.

When I opened my eyes, she was smiling at me, probably thinking along the same lines. I didn't want to break the silent spell the city had held over us. I brought out the mixed leaves, making sure there were enough of all four types to put into each of the muslin bags later. For now, I just put the leaves in a pile between us.

I lit the silver candle and looked up. Hannah nodded. I passed the candle from my right hand to her left, then she passed it to her right, and finally she passed it around to my left. We sent the silver candle with its flame around three times as I spoke:

What was lost or stolen shall come circling back to rest
Just as magic circles round, may dreams be put to test.
Visions, dreams within our sleep, tell us what we need.
Let the wisdom of the moon help to plant the seed.

We sat again in silence, then heard the familiar voice of Sedona behind Hannah.

"No, no, don't bother waiting for little old meeee-ow," she said. "That sounded like a good one, though. Still on the great chintzy bracelet mystery, Nancy Drew and Trixie Belden?" She tiptoed up to Hannah and nonchalantly brushed up against her, purring.

She kids around a lot with Hannah, too.

"Yes, and you can help, Miss Sedona," Hannah said, scratching the cat under her chin. "Maddie just cast a dream and wisdom spell, so all of us can put our little bags under our pillows tonight, and we can log our dreams in our journals—oh, wait. You need opposable thumbs to write, I'm sorry, Sedona. You'll have to just try to remember your dreams."

"Very furry. I mean funny," Sedona answered. "I'll have you know I remember every one of my dreams and have no need for a journal, thank you. Now if you'll just give me a moment, I have a story to tell you."

"Not now, Sedona," I said. It's not story time up here. We're trying to concentrate to make sure the dream spell works.

"But––"

"But whatever the story, Sedona, it can wait."

After a stare-off with me, Sedona turned and pussyfooted to the ledge of the rooftop. She bounded up to it and stuck her head between two spokes of the wrought iron railing that enclosed us.

"Oh look," she said, with a backward glance over her shoulder. "Some fine-looking gentleman who used to wear a police uniform has come to join our little party. Only now he's wearing...um...comfies."

Chapter 19: Dream Police

Officer Miles Denton looked up at the three of us, all gathered at the ledge of the rooftop. He waved at us. I waved back, kind of limp-wristed and feeling that old adrenaline rush again. The man just did something to me. Magic of his own.

He motioned for me, or I guess us, to come down and I gave him the finger. Not that finger, the index one, the "wait a minute" one. He gave me two thumbs up. Already, it's like we had this secret little language, just us two.

"Hey, he's cute!" Hannah said as she followed me inside. We took the elevator and didn't notice until too late that Sedona had been walking too slowly to keep up with us. She'd have to catwalk around ledges again and take the fire escape on the other side of the building in order to get to her open window downstairs. She wasn't going to be happy.

I straightened my sweatshirt under my dirty work apron as much as I could and took deep yoga breaths.

"Cute? Officer Denton? I hardly noticed, because, you know me. I don't really base much on appearances. But like I told you today, he has a certain amount of cute to him, sure. If you're into that kind of cute, I mean," I said demurely. But when I looked at Hannah, she was giving me that puckered-lips-to-the-side look. She knew I was into this kind of cute.

"Officer Denton! How are you tonight?" I stepped out of our building and stuck out my hand. Stupid, right? Like a police officer, even one in plain clothes, needs to shake hands every time he sees you.

But the thing is, he took my hand. Maybe because he was off duty and he seemed like a whole new person. Anyway, he took my hand and he squeezed. And he looked right into my eyes, and his eyes were like big old chocolate drops that I just wanted to swim in. I know my smile was probably goofy, but there are some moments in life when you just don't have control. So be it.

"Ms. Bridges. Maddie," he said. And he gave me a goofy smile right back! I swear.

"Hannah, meet Officer Miles Denton, apparently wandering the dark and dangerous streets even while off duty. And Offi–Miles, this is my best friend, Hannah Balauru. She's a psychic. She owns *Seeing is Believing*, up the street. You probably know all this stuff."

"Well, I'm still pretty new to this precinct," he said, still smiling with those white, white teeth. "Even if I knew it before, it's always good to review." He shook Hannah's hand and I noticed he didn't squeeze hers nearly as hard as he squeezed mine. I ran my fingers through my hair. I must look a mess at this hour.

"What's going on up there on the roof?" he asked, jerking his chin up. Sedona was still up on the ledge and I could tell she was pissed. Her tail made really fast jerking twitches. I waved at her with an apologetic smile on my face.

"We were just conjuring up some possibilities," I said. "That's my cat, Sedona."

He made as if to wave up at her and froze mid-wave when her little front paw came up and waved back down at him.

"Did she—"

"Wave at you?" I interjected. "She did! It's a new trick. She's full of them." We looked at each other for just a moment longer than necessary, and then he relaxed his waving arm.

"Wow. I didn't know you could train a cat."

"You can't," I answered. "It's more like the other way around. But she thought this would impress me, so there it is." I shrugged and gave a strangled little laugh.

Hannah cleared her throat. "I should get going, Maddie. Officer, nice to meet you, and I hope you'll stop into my shop one day." She turned on her heel, but Miles stopped her.

"Wait, Hannah is it? I had some questions. It's about Ms. Esther's, uh, robbery. And I'd rather have the two of you together for this, if that's okay. I'd appreciate anything you both could offer. I know it's late, but…" He looked back and forth at each of us, nibbling on his lower lip. I felt my stomach drop.

We had an awkward moment of silence until I finally figured out that since we were in front of my apartment building, then maybe I should be inviting them inside. My stomach lurched, thinking about the cat hair everywhere, and my dirty clothes strewn all over my bed and the smell of salmon and the dishes in the sink, well, all of it. You know the feeling.

"Won't you come in for a glass of water, Officer? Or gosh, since the uniform's gone, maybe even a beer? We just need to collect our things from the roof and you're free to come with!" I flashed a casual enough grin and he followed us into the elevator to the roof.

We gathered the holly, ash, and bay leaves together, Hannah and I each scraping a little handful to place into the muslin bags. Miles watched us in silence for a minute, then turned his back on us. He stood like a statue of Apollo, looking down at the street.

"Tell me, are you practicing?" he asked, still not turning toward us. "Or are you just playing at it?"

Well, I didn't quite know what to do with those questions. Hannah, though, remember, she's a psychic. She knew exactly where he was in his thoughts.

"Tell him the truth," she whispered, still squatting by the site of our spell, smelling her dream bag.

"No!" I hissed back through my teeth.

"Yes!" said Officer Miles Denton.

We both looked up at him and he extended his hand down toward me.

"It's okay, Maddie," he said. "Really." I took his hand and he helped me to my feet, pulled me closer than he needed to, if you ask me, and his smile, now fading, was turning into a straight, grim line.

"Um," I said, trying to look him in the eye, "we were, uh, practicing, I guess you would say." I chanced a quick look up into his eyes, and they were filled with...what, doubt? Sadness? Anger, even?

"That's what I thought," he said, looking down at the street, "and I've had an inkling ever since I met you this morning." He must have seen a shadow of worry cross my face, because his hand squeezed mine right before he dropped it like it was a tarantula. I felt my heart leap up in my chest.

"So," he said, again looking down at the street. "You're

witches."

Chapter 20: It's Complicated

"You know, Miles…we're okay now with me calling you Miles, right?" I watched the corners of his mouth twitch a little, which gave me some encouragement. He gave a terse nod and I continued, "Well, Miles, witches aren't the evil-hearted creatures that the cartoons and books make them out to be. We're just people who believe we can make the world, or at least ourselves, better through our beliefs and our intentions."

Hannah chipped in. "Some of us are healers, some of us work with spirits that most people can no longer communicate with. It's all a matter of hard work mixed with natural abilities." She paused, curling a dreadlock around her index finger. "And really, it's a totally legal practice. Um, sir." She giggled a little and I threw her the stink eye.

"Yes," Miles said, looking first at Hannah then back at me. "I've had my share of experience with witchcraft, and while we don't need to go into all that right now, I can assure you I won't be, ah, asking too many questions about it. Unless it turns out to have something to do with this case. I just have a few questions, so if you don't mind?" He made a motion toward the door.

I looked down at my little muslin bags and cleared my throat. "Of course. Where are my manners? Shall we? It looks like rain." We climbed down the stairs from the rooftop and I tried not to think about his words. I tend to talk when I'm trying to keep my mind off of unpleasant things, but tonight felt different.

I felt like I'd been rejected up on my roof, spurned because of who and what I was, and the adrenaline rush from realizing that Miles obviously had some kind of issue with witchcraft had subsided, leaving me feeling deflated and hopeless. I had to work hard to cover up my hurt feelings, to change my thinking about what had just transpired into a 'no big deal' moment. "A beer for your trouble? I flashed him a tentative smile.

"Oh, no, but thanks," he answered. "This won't take that long."

Blown it. I had totally blown it.

Or had I? Suddenly a little defiant wave of anger rose up in me. He might not want to get involved with me because of what I was, but dammit, I didn't want anything to do with him if he had negative feelings toward me, either, right?

"Right!" I said, and he thought I was answering him, when really it was just that very constant conversation with myself that was coming out. "No matter," I continued. "We'll just do our best to help Ms. Esther, and you can be out the door!" Maybe I sounded a bit too enthusiastic to get rid of him. "Good!" I answered myself.

Back in the apartment, I threw a few sweaters from the couch to the bedroom, got us some water and hoped Sedona would either stay away or be on her good behavior. She'd already left the roof by the time we got up there, and I whispered a silent apologetic spell, hoping for the best. I'd been on her bad side so many times lately that I just couldn't be sure whether she would embarrass me or not. Although by this time, really, who cared if she was completely herself around Officer Denton? That cat was most certainly out of the bag anyway, so to speak.

"So? You have questions?" I perched beside him on the couch, where he had made himself comfortable.

"I do," he said. "First, do you remember exactly what time Ms. Sena came into your shop this morning? To tell you about the robbery?" He pulled a little black notebook out and flipped it open.

"Hmm," I said, closing my eyes. "Yes, I'm saying it was just after 11:00? The shop was open, and I was charm–I mean, I was feeding my plants in the back. Why?"

"And she said that her apartment had been broken into just then?" he asked, ignoring my question. "While she was at bingo?"

"That's right," I said. I closed my eyes and held my little bag of herbs up to my nose.

"And you know for a fact that her bingo games are in the mornings?"

"Hmm. She's mentioned these morning sessions, but she has St. Joe's, too. They have bingo a few times a week, I think, around dinner time. I'd say bingo's all over the board, so to speak." My eyes fluttered open and I caught Hannah's smirk out of the corner of my eye.

"That's fine, I'm just going down every possible road, here," he said. He was taking notes, but not really. I can read upside down, and the marks he was putting down on that little Moleskine weren't real words. Doodles, maybe.

"Why, Officer?" Hannah interjected. "What are you thinking? That Esther might be lying? About the robbery? Or where she had been?"

"No, no," he answered. "It's kind of complicated, actually. We had a call tonight from Mrs. Sena's neighbor, a Mr. Lloyd Benson? That name ring a bell with either of you?"

I gulped. "Well, sure! He lives across the hall from Ms. Esther. I just felt him…er, or rather, I sensed him…I guess you could say that I 'saw' him in his apartment tonight, peeking out his door at us when we came home from Hannah's shop. Why?"

"I'm not at liberty to go into details, Ms.–"

"Maddie. Please." I gave him an ingratiating smile and hoped I didn't have basil between my teeth.

"Maddie. I know I'll get used to that, sorry." He gave me the smile and I felt a very involuntary plummet of my innards. "I know you're trying to help us out on this case," Miles said. "But I'll caution you. The police have the capability to handle it, and quite frankly, the kind of help you have to offer just might backfire on us all and muddy the waters. Please know that I believe that you are not culpable in this break-in, but, uh…" He licked his bottom lip and I licked mine. "Your name has actually come up in the course of the investigation, after all."

I felt the adrenaline rush through me, but this time it was a bad rush, not a crush rush. I decided to pretend he hadn't even said that last sentence. "Well, the fact is, Miles, that I *do* have certain powers. Intuitions, you could call them. And while you might have issues with what I'm sure must have been misguided magic in your personal experience, my own gifts have come to me naturally, as well as after hard and thorough study. I can assure you that my contributions to the case are very apt to pleasantly surprise you. And your Sergeant." Lost in my own words, I finally caught my breath and looked at him.

I could tell. I could just tell that he was fighting a smile.

"I know," I continued, "you're all busy with way bigger fish in your sea than this little robbery. Gods know New York can be nasty. So really, yes, I'd like to pitch in here, because Ms. Esther is a friend and a neighbor. But also because I feel a little responsible, to tell you the truth."

"You feel responsible?" he asked, and suddenly he started writing, I mean really writing words in his notebook. "Like how?"

"Oh, I don't mean I did anything wrong, here, Miles, sir Miles," See? I hate this, when my words get all mixed up. It's something I'm working on. My mouth just tends to work about a beat ahead of my brain. It's frustrating.

"I just mean," I clarified, slowing down my lips with concentration, "that I have kind of a protective ward, or um, shield, if you will, on my building. And somehow that shield didn't work this morning. Or whenever the robbery actually occurred. Or," I stopped, considering this for the first time, "perhaps my shield didn't work because the thief is someone I assumed to be completely harmless."

Chapter 21: Talk to Me

Whew. The thing about being a witch is that it's a very, very difficult thing to explain to non-witches. Really, most of us are very pure. Working with solid intention for the greater good of all, our spells more often than not are based in clarifying what puzzles, easing what strains, relaxing what is tense. We look to help others sleep well, be of good cheer and find the gratitude in their lives.

In some people's vocabularies, the word "witch" is linked to green wart-nosed black-hatted women on brooms, women who cast evil spells on innocents, and cackle at the full moon with their potions and steaming kettles, their black cats on the ready for a quick getaway.

With most people, people who aren't witches, it's a tough subject to discuss. Usually it didn't make any difference at all to me, what other people thought when it came to who and what I was. This felt different, like a low-grade fever. I wanted Miles Denton to approve of me, accept me, and from the tone of his voice up on the roof, it sounded like that wish of mine might be too big of a challenge.

Sedona strolled into the room, tail still flicking. I could tell she was still put off from us leaving her up on the roof. I offered my splayed fingers to her, which usually works as an apology. She loves rubbing against them like a hairbrush, but this time she just gave me the slow blink.

Don't talk, don't talk, don't talk, I screamed at her inside my head. Another slow blink and she jumped up on my lap, grabbed one of my muslin bags of dreams in her mouth and leaped back down and out of the room.

"Hey!" I shouted. "I'm sorry, Miles, be right back." I followed Sedona into the kitchen.

"Give that back," I hissed at her once the door was closed.

She spit the bag out. "You have dissed me. Too. Many. Times. I'm a cat, for gods' sakes, Madeline. No opposable thumbs. Now, I don't ask for much around here. A little fish, some nice treats, a drop of cream now and then, keep a door open for me once in a while. But I'm asking. Telling you now. Respect me. Or I will talk in front of that hunk of delicious semi-sweet chocolate out there and make your little crush crumble right in front of you. Hear me?"

I sighed and picked up my dream bag.

"I hear you, Sedona. And I'm sorry. I apologize. You're right." I leaned down and she let me touch her behind her one ear. "Sometimes I just assume that since you're a cat, you kind of enjoy walking the ledges, and I know I've been shutting a lot of doors in your face these past couple of days."

"I could contribute to your little investigation, you know. Take tonight, for exam–" she said.

"I know, I know. But right now? I have a policeman. I mean, I have a policeman in my living room. So we'll talk later, okay? Promise." I opened the fridge and dug a little tuna out of an open can. "Peace?"

Sedona's mind just shuts down in the presence of food. Even if she had just eaten and bathed, she would still be game for a snack. Her ears went up and that was that. She got lost in the tuna and I left her there. Turns out I accidentally closed the kitchen door on my way back to the living room.

"Sorry," I said as I settled back on the couch.

"What's in those bags, anyway?" Miles asked, looking from Hannah's to mine.

"They're dream sachets," Hannah jumped in. "They're for under our pillows tonight, to help us see more clearly. Our dreams might just lead us to who stole Ms. Esther's bracelet." She blushed a little as I glared at her. Now she'd opened the can of worms and he'd think I was a crazy. Crazier.

"And you burned things up on the roof to make them?" he asked, still writing in his book.

"We just used candles, Officer," I said, pointedly not using his first name. "No actual 'fires.' And no, nothing was burned. The candle was just for," I cast around, looking for careful words, "added peace."

"Ah," he said.

"But to get back to Mr. Benson?" I said. "I know you can't say what he called about earlier, but did you need anything else from me? Us? About him?"

"Well, sure, if you have anything to add, now's the time." He looked up through long black eyelashes from his doodles, and my breath caught in my throat.

"Asking Maddie to add things to a conversation, now, that's asking for problems," said Sedona, who had found her way here from the kitchen, probably by slipping out the window, around the ledge, and through the open bedroom window. Now she had jumped up to the arm of Hannah's chair.I felt anger and maybe just a touch of panic pump through me. Sedona was throwing me a haughty glare, but Hannah's mouth was open, so Miles seemed to assume that the voice had been hers, even though they sound nothing alike. Hannah has a very pronounced Brooklyn accent, and Sedona, well, Sedona practices her enunciation in front of my vanity mirror every day in order to escape any kind of accent at all.

Officer Denton looked back at me and I stammered, "Well, okay, yes, so I tend to chatter a bit, I suppose. But most people seem to kind of enjoy it, I think, um, Hannah. Usually my talk is about them, anyway. 'People love to talk about themselves.' That's what Broderick Moore from *The Fossil Store* always used to say. Broderick Moore and Dale Carnegie, of course."

There was a very definite silence in the room. I took advantage. "As I said earlier, I met Lloyd Benson, formally, I mean, yesterday. Ms. Esther thinks he has a crush on her. Says he watches her every move when she's out there in the hall. He usually goes to bingo with her, but he 'didn't feel up to bingo' today." I made air quotes to make it legit.

"Hmm," Miles said. "Well, he called the station this evening, as I said. Asked questions about whether any other elderly folks have shown up at the station lately. Asked very specifically about a few of your older neighbors, all women."

"Did he ask about Ms. Esther?" I asked.

"No, the notes I saw tonight in my email said he just wanted to touch base about her robbery, just to see if there was anything we might need from him. I'm going to give him a call tomorrow, just to, well, frankly, just to include him. What I really wanted to ask of you two," he said, putting the tip of his pen into the corner of his mouth, "was more along the line of whether you know anything about Ms. Esther's personal life."

"Well, I've been trying to tell you all night, but you've been busy chasing your own tail, Maddie." Her tail twitched. "It's about that Mrs. Peterson woman who lives down the street. Old lady, she's been in the shop a couple of times. Bent almost in two because of the hump on her back. Looks like a shelf bracket? You know who I'm talking about?"

"Peterson?!" Miles Denton practically shouted.

"Peterson?" I asked at exactly the same moment. We looked at each other and I almost said, "Jinx!" but I didn't want him any more spooked than he already was.

"Why does that name mean anything to you?" I asked him.

"Never mind," he answered. "It's confidential. It's business. It's…"

"Wait," I interrupted. "The only Peterson I know is the woman who was at the station at the same time as me, yesterday morning. The one who was complaining about the construction guys and the landlord. Maybe you hadn't come out to the front desk yet." I closed my eyes to look back at my memories.

"Was she all stooped over?" Hannah asked.

"Yes, she was. She's been in the shop several times. I kind of sort of recognized her." I visualized Mrs. Peterson again. "And hey! She wrote her address down for Chief Whatshisname, MilkCarton, and the piece of paper she wrote it on got accidentally swept into my carpetbag!" I was getting really excited now. This couldn't all just be coincidence.

"And what's more," said Hannah, who was waving her hand in the air like a fourth-grader who knew the answer in class, "is that she, Mrs. Peterson, must be the old lady who appeared to me right before the lucky bingo troll as the séance was wearing away!"

We all stopped, stunned.

"Excuse me?" Sedona was down on the floor at this point, stretching. Her front claws were extended into my area rug and she was pulling her body away from them.

She yawned. "I know this seems crazy, but perhaps we could take turns. Talking, I mean. Far be it from me, a *talking cat*, to try to steal the show, but hey, all you have," she looked at me, "is a piece of paper with an address. And you," she looked at Hannah, "all you have is a wisp of a dream state. And you, tall, dark, and purrrfect," she turned delicately to face Miles, "have nothing to offer, since you're busy keeping secrets."

It was an awkward moment, but I love awkward moments. They tend to be the spice in those slide show memories.

"Okay, shoot," Miles said. He took a deep pull from his beer and picked up his notebook again.

"You see, Officer, being a cat offers a unique opportunity to me. I get to listen to all kinds of conversations and slip inside all kinds of windows and sometimes doors," Sedona gave me a sideways smirk, "that would be closed to me if I were human. When I was so rudely locked up here earlier this evening, I needed to take the ledges and landings approach to get up to the rooftop, which means my first stop was the window on second. It's the only window you can count on to be open all the time, although sometimes that lady on four, what's her name, Marian something? No, Martha? Anyway, sometimes she leaves the fourth-floor window open, but there's just no guarantee—"

"Sedona! Get to the point!" I had the strangest feeling that she was trying to draw this out just to get back at us for all the times I'd let her down.

"Ah. Well, I saw Mrs. Peterson. Running from Esther Sena's

apartment. Well, if you could call that little scuttle a run. She had a frightening look on her face. She left the door ajar, so I went in, thinking maybe some of those boxes on her counter may be open. Her door was still open, after all, and how do I know when my next bite will be these days?"

I rolled my eyes and my head fell back on the couch.

"Hmm," said Miles. So Mrs. Peterson was visiting Mrs. Sena tonight." He scribbled a few words down.

"But that's just the first chapter of that story," said Sedona. "Later, when I was so rudely locked up on the roof," and here she sent a glare my way, "I had to stop on that floor again to get my bearings after all those greasy fire escapes from six to five, then those skinny ledges between four and three--"

"Sedona!" I just about shouted.

"Yes," she said very softly. "I stopped once again at Ms. Esther's place, call it a cat's curiosity, hmm? Never know what you've left behind. And the door, well, it was still open."

I was ready to explode. "Just get to it, if there even is a point, Sedona! Ms. Esther was there, wasn't she? She should have been sleeping by then. What time do you think this was?" I picked up my phone and studied it, playing with time inside my head.

"Oh, she was in there all right," Sedona answered. "But she wasn't sleeping."

"What do you mean?" Miles asked.

"I mean," said Sedona, and she licked her left paw, leaving a deliberately dramatic silence, "that Esther Sena is dead."

Chapter 23: Dead End

After that initial blast of stunned silence, we all of course rushed downstairs to Ms. Esther's place. It was late, or early, I guess, so we kept our voices low, but I was sure all of her neighbors would be sleeping anyway.

Sure enough, her door was open, just as Sedona had said. All the lights were out, and there lay Ms. Esther, in her bed with the nightlight glowing at her side. The sheets were all twisted and lay in messy piles on top of her, but she herself looked composed and peaceful. Ms. Esther had either passed away like that proverbial best death scenario, just sleeping away, or...

"...or she was murdered," I said aloud.

"Was that the back end of the convo that's just happening inside your head?" Hannah smiled at me in appreciation.

"Yeah, sorry," I said. "I'm thinking maybe she just slept away? Surely some people actually do that, right?" I peered over Miles' shoulder as he felt Ms. Esther's throat for a pulse.

"The lucky ones, yes," Miles said. "But since this whole day has been about Ms. Esther Sena, we can't assume anything. We need to not touch anything. Hey!" He had turned and was pointing a finger at Sedona, who was out in the kitchen, sniffing along the counter for leftovers. "Get down from there, right now!" He swallowed when he saw her fiery eyes glaring at him. "I mean, please. Please try not to sully the scene. Come on, everyone. I'll call the station and we'll let the experts handle the rest."

I still had Ms. Esther's key in my pocket, and when I touched it, a lump formed in my throat. Did we really need to lock the door behind us? It wasn't as if we needed to keep Ms. Esther safe. As I started to follow the others in the hall, dragging my feet and trying not to cry, I felt that weird raised-hair thing, and stopped right in front of Mr. Benson's door. I just stood there, waiting.

He caved too easily. After just a minute, Mr. Benson's front door cracked open and his beady eyes blinked at me.

"Why are you here so late?" he asked.

"Why are you watching out your peephole so late?" I asked.

"What's going on over there?" he asked.

"What do you think is going on over here?" I asked.

I was pretty good at the interrogation end of investigative work.

But maybe not. He slammed the door shut and I felt him drift away. I knocked ever so gently. No sense waking anyone else. When he opened up again, he let me see a good solid four inches of his face.

"Mr. Benson, the police are going to be coming pretty soon. They might appreciate you telling them anything you know about what's gone on here with Ms. Sena these last two days.

"Why can't they just talk to Esther herself?"

"They might appreciate as many points of view as possible."

"Oh." He seemed to consider this, maybe with a touch of

relief, then nodded. "Okay. I'm a night owl, so I'll be up anyway. I did notice, now that you mention it, that Esther's door was ajar earlier...thought maybe she'd gone down to grab her mail or whatnot. Give the police my apartment number?" He was acting all nonchalant, like maybe I didn't know Ms. Esther was dead. Like maybe I didn't know he'd already called the station tonight.

"You bet." I gave a narrow-eyed glare to the sliver of his face and walked fast to catch up with Hannah and Miles. Let him squirm. If he murdered Ms. Esther, he'd be peering out from between bars someday soon, that was for sure. Miles and his team were sure to get to the bottom of this. Maybe with a little of my help.

"Where's Sedona?" I asked Hannah.

"Flew the coop. Jumped out that window." She nodded toward the hallway window, open just about a foot, exactly as Sedona had described earlier. "What are you thinking, Maddie? Because I can't help but wonder about that little Mrs. Peterson, you know? Sedona saw her running from Esther's apartment tonight, for gods' sakes! Plus, she came to me in my vision after the séance. And on top of it all, your policeman acted kind of weird about her name tonight. She has to be at the very heart of this whole thing, right?" She had a thick dread of blond hair in her mouth and was nervously nibbling on it. I raised my lip.

"Ick, Hannah. Stop with the hair."

"Oh. Sorry. Habit."

Miles was waiting for us, leaning against my apartment door, texting. He looked up and caught my eye, and a genuine expression of concern passed over his face. He cleared his throat.

"You ladies okay? I know that was probably a shock, to see

her that way."

I opened my door to lead them inside at the same time I opened my mouth to tell him I was okay, but Hannah was already talking.

"Oh, we don't worry too much about death, to tell you the truth," she was saying. "Witches know that death is just a passageway, that there is more to our existence than our mortal bodies. We know, deep in the fibers of our beings, that Ms. Esther is still a very real essence, and that we could join her in conversation and feast anytime we'd like to visit. Isn't that right, Maddie?"

I sighed. Truth be told, some deaths, my father's among them, had hit me about as hard and laid me about as low as if I were any non-witch human. I got what she was saying about our philosophies, but it's a lot easier to say than to practice, the nonchalant acceptance of the passing from our world to the next.

But for now, I went along. "Pretty much wraps it up, there, Hannah. Thanks for summing it up for our kind and unsuspecting neighborhood policeman." I smiled at him with a taste of chagrin in my mouth, but his eyes had taken back that sparkle.

"Well, to tell you the truth, I already knew all that stuff, Hannah. But thank you for the review. For now, suffice it to say that as with all cases that have a possible criminality to them, all persons of interest should be aware that they are being investigated. So that means, unfortunately, that you will both..." He trailed off, and I knew exactly what was swirling around in his head.

"Sedona," I said. "What are you going to do about her? Does she count as a 'Person of Interest?'" I made the sarcastic air quotes sign.

He just stared at us both for a couple of seconds.

"No. No, there's no way a cat could murder someone. She can't even open a window by herself, right? No, let's just agree we won't mention Sedona." He grabbed his notebook out of his back pocket and started paging through it. We watched him as he ripped out two of the pages, crumpled them up, and stuffed them into his front pocket.

I smiled up at him. "Our little secret, Officer Denton. Right, Hannah? You can count on us."

"Um. I don't know," Hannah said, and that stupid strand of hair went back into her mouth. It's like she needs to suck on her hair in order to think or something. Drives me mad.

"Thing is," she said, "that I'm a really, really, honest person?" I'd been noticing lately that when Hannah gets nervous, all her sentences end up sounding like questions. I bit the inside of my cheek as she went on. "Like, I can tell this story and not mention that Sedona was the one who told us Esther was dead? But then how are we supposed to twist the truth into something that would make sense and not have us flunk all kinds of lie detector tests?"

Well, she had us there.

"Sedona only talks to non-witches if she's really angry or she has something really important to say," I said, looking at Miles and suddenly feeling nervous. I turned back to Hannah. "She won't cooperate and just sit down for a nice conversation with the cops. It's just not in her."

I looked back at Miles. "You'll look like a crazy person if you tell them the cat told you Ms. Esther was dead. Or they'll smell your breath and think, 'Hmm, wonder why Miles Denton is at the scene of a crime, off duty, and drinking beer with a couple of the suspects? After midnight?'"

I had run out of breath.

"What do we say, then?" Miles was starting to shift his weight from one foot to the other, over and over. "I'm new to the precinct, damn it! I can't be caught in the witchcraft web! Not again! His eyes were wide open, and they glanced back and forth between Hannah and me. His lips were dry. Worst of all, he was starting to make that awful dry mouth sound that's like fingernails on chalkboard to me.

"What do you mean, *again*?" Sedona asked as she slowly came around the corner. She landed on the sofa's arm again and blinked her slow blink at Miles. "You're 'caught in the witchcraft web. Again?'"

"Never mind," he mumbled. He reached into his back pocket and brought out a pack of gum. "It's a long story, and someday we'll all sit around and drink one of your lovely cups of tea and I'll tell it, okay? But in the meantime, we have to—"

He stopped talking when my buzzer went off. Someone was down at the street level. Miles shielded his eyes from the lights' glare to look through my window.

"It's a couple guys from the force," he said, chomping on his gum. "We tell them this: I got the email at home about Benson calling in, decided to take a walk past your building, you happened to be outside, I questioned you, had a beer because I'm off duty, and we went downstairs with your key to Esther Sena's apartment just to check on her. After your whatever."

"Séance," Hannah said with a smile as she pressed my buzzer.

"Whatever. Okay, séance." Miles took a deep breath, blew into his cupped hand and opened my door.

I took the liberty, couldn't help it. I reached out to touch his hand and felt a little zap of electricity. "And Officer," I said, "those words you just said? They sound like the truth to me. Except for leaving out the talking cat, I mean."

Chapter 24: Long Day's Journey into Night

Two cops came into my apartment, sizing it up. I tried to see it fresh, through investigators' eyes.

My apartment is alive with color: the kitchen is painted pumpkin-orange, the living room is a soft sage with deep forest green area rugs, my bedroom is red, womb red. On the walls are photographs I had taken myself, all in different sizes, all botanical.

I liked getting up close and personal with plants, of course, so the ferns and dandelions and spores were all blown up, and all three rooms displayed the plants I loved and plants I had met by accident, out on beaches or in parks.

Their names, the cops, that is, not the plants, were Koester and Plack. They were both obviously having love affairs with sugar and fat, and probably beer. Their pudgy faces were splotched with red, so who knows? Maybe wine instead of beer. Maybe both. Their heads swiveled around, taking in my plant pictures, squinting in the brilliance of my kitchen, then settling on the wings of my owl clock.

Officer Denton stood by my door, shifting his weight and

breathing big gulps of air as he chomped his gum. I stifled the smile that was busting to cross my face.

There had been a death, after all. Smiling people weren't appropriate here.

"You two are personal friends, then?" Officer Koester seemed to be the one in charge, and after introductions, he walked back to my door and opened it, jerking his chin out toward the hall and throwing a meaningful glance at Miles and Plack.

"Ms. Esther and me, you mean?" I asked. "Well, yes, we're neighbors, as you can see," I said, "and Ms. Esther is, um, was, my landlady. And a steady customer down in my shop. That's my shop downstairs. She loves my tea. Loved. She loved my tea." For the second time that night, a knot found its way into my throat.

"Yes, ma'am," Officer Plack said. He casually plucked something from just inside one of his nostrils with his thumb, then nodded at Koester. "We'll just go sit with her until the folks from the morgue get here. No need for you ladies to revisit the scene. We'll give you a call in the morning?" His eyes searched Koester's and he licked his lips that were already so cracked and sore looking I almost reached for a stem of aloe for him to use as a balm. "And then we'll be in touch about maybe you coming down to the station for just a few questions?"

Hannah and I both nodded at them, and Miles took a last look at us before leaving. I grabbed one of my muslin bags from my pocket and shoved it into his hand as I shook it good-bye.

"Put this under your pillow tonight and as soon as you wake up, write down anything, and I mean anything, that you can remember about your dreams," I whispered. I gave his hand and the bag another quick squeeze and tried to not sweat onto him.

He cleared his throat and shot a glance down my hall at the other cops. "Ms. Bridges, Ms. Belauru, I thank you both for your assistance tonight." He tucked the bag into his front pocket and met my eyes just as the door closed between us.

It was like I could almost see through the door; his stare was that tangible. His eyes, meeting mine, was just this magical feeling that had nothing to do with my being a witch. There was something there, something palpable that made me want to throw that door back open and race after him down the hall. Anything, just to touch that hand again.

"We have some work to do here, Maddie." Hannah was pacing along the edge of my area rug, as if she were measuring the room. Heel to toe, like she was on a balance beam or a tightwire. Such an odd duck, I thought as I watched her with her gross little dreadlock in her mouth. But she was my odd duck, and I was sincerely grateful to the universe for Hannah Belauru. I loved having her in my life.

"Yes," I said. "You want a drink? Sedona!" I called. "You can come out now! We have some things to discuss, and you need to be a part of it!" She must have taken cover under the bed.

"I'd love a water, thanks," Hannah said.

"And I'd love a saucer of heavy cream. Cream so heavy it'll knock me out for a solid nine hours, please." Sedona slid into the room from the bedroom.

After I'd brought our drinks in, we all cozied up under blankets on the couch, Hannah's feet flat up against mine, Sedona curled up under my legs.

"What I don't get," said Hannah, her eyes closed and her head resting on the arm of my sofa, "is this Hester Esther mix up. Poor old Harry. Maddie, you should have heard him. So confused. He was asking why in the world Hester would be coming to a medium just to talk to an old dead boyfriend who gave her a bracelet decades ago."

"Yeah, the name game is tricky in this case, that's for sure," I said. Sedona's purring was loud and steady now, a nice mix with the ticking of my wall clock's second wing. The owl's eyes were still open. Such a grand time of day, unless death was involved.

"I can't believe she's dead," I said after my own eyes had been closed for a minute's silence.

"Sure you can, Maddie," Sedona purred.

"But we were just talking to her dead husband! Like, *hours* ago!" This, I've noticed, is something lots of us do; we find it hard to fathom, that someone could be consciously with us one moment, and then gone from our world the next. As if talking with them earlier discounted death's possibility altogether.

I took a cleansing breath and returned to the living and the problems living presented. "Well, ladies," I said, "What we have are the following pieces of our puzzle: a troll with blue hair, an old woman who's bent over and showing up as a vision at the séance, a missing bracelet, a nosy peeping Benson neighbor who called the station tonight but we don't know why, an old girlfriend whose name rhymes with the victim's, the victim's dead husband who said he'd see her soon, and the victim herself, now deceased. Oh," I said after a nudge from my conscience, "also a mysterious but beautiful pair of earrings that might have been buried in a certain philodendron who was suffering intolerable lack of light and water in said victim's abode."

"Earrings? I haven't heard anything about earrings," said Hannah, sitting up.

"Yeah, I found them when I accidentally pushed the plant out my window while I was spying on Officer Miles," I said with a smile. "They were mixed in with the dirt on the street when I went down to save him."

"Save him? You think Officer Denton needed to be saved?"

"No, you bean. I had to run down to save Phil! The plant!" We both laughed, but then stopped at the same time. There was something inappropriate about laughing on the night one of your neighbors gets killed. Or dies naturally. Whichever.

"And don't forget that strange, bent-over lady, Mrs. Peterson, sneaking into Esther's apartment," Sedona said from under the blanket. "We *are* assuming that she's the same woman who showed up at the séance, all bent over, right?"

"Assume, assume, you know what they say about it, Sedona, my friend," said Hannah, rubbing her eyes. "I'm beat, guys. Let's sleep on the pieces, and oh, while we're at it, let's sleep with our dream bags pinned to the pillows, right? And hey, why did we make four bags anyway? I get the three, one for Sedona, one for each of us."

"Oh, the extra is usually to leave as an anchor, on the altar. But I wanted Miles to dream tonight..." I let my finger trail along the rough edges of my bag.

"Hmm," said Sedona. "Sounds fishy to me."

I ignored her. "Before you leave, can we just try to get a quick check-in with Ms. Esther? Do you mind, Hannah?" I knew you needed three for a séance, but who knew, maybe Sedona would count in this instance. I roused her from her cozy position between us, and she begrudgingly sat up.

We each placed a hand on one of her paws to form a circle, well, a sort of circle, and we closed our eyes. Silently, we meditated our good thoughts toward our newly passed friend, and I don't know about Hannah, but I felt like Ms. Esther was right in that room with us, maybe not ready to converse just yet, but I felt her just the same.

"Esther, if you can hear me," Hannah said, very softly so she wouldn't jar Ms. Esther's newly dead nerves, "please know that we make several promises to you tonight. We promise first of all to find out who killed you, if someone killed you. We promise to find any loved ones you might have, maybe an attorney? Yikes, Maddie, we hardly know Ms. Esther—"

"Shhh," I said, shaking my head.

"And lastly, Esther," she went on, "We promise to find that bracelet."

There was a silence then, and I worried for a moment that Hannah had maybe fallen asleep.

"Oh, you know it, girlfriend!" Sedona suddenly blurted out. "You are humming a few bars of my favorite tuna!"

"Shush! Sedona!" I hissed. She was interrupting our flow and the possibility of a connection.

"It's okay, Maddie," said Hannah. "I'm pretty sure it's too soon to expect any two-way communication with Esther anyway." She scratched Sedona's ears, a little too hard, if you asked me. "What in the world were you talking about, anyway, KitKat?"

"Esther wanted me to make sure I helped clean out her refrigerator," Sedona said. "She just reminded me that she went to the fish market yesterday after bingo. She has fresh *Yellowfin* in there."

She gave me a disdainful look. "And all *you* could find was deli meat and cheese that smells like butt."

Chapter 25: Dreams to Remember

Sedona flicked her tail and watched through slit eyes as I finished getting ready for bed that night. She loved having something she could hold over Hannah and me, I think, especially when it involved magic. She had never, to my knowledge, communicated with anyone in the spirit world, so what had happened earlier between Ms. Esther and Sedona was a huge magical deal. Something that could have erupted jealousy or at least envy in me.

At that point, though, I didn't even care; I was drop-dead exhausted, excuse the pun, and just wanted to plummet head-first into dreams. Hopefully they wouldn't be break-out-in-a-sweat dreams.

I pinned my little muslin bag to the bottom of my pillow, then stopped to consider. Would it be so awful, really, if I slipped a stem of True Jasmine into my bag? Jasmine was a sure-fire ingredient if you wanted to have dreams about your romantic interest. I grew it as a houseplant in my kitchen and sold it during the season as an outdoor trellis vine.

I tiptoed into the kitchen and thanked Jas kindly as I pinched off just the tiniest sprig from one of her stems. On the way back into the bedroom, I stopped to touch the earrings that I'd found on the sidewalk. They might come in handy tonight, I thought. I took one back to bed with me. Then I stuffed the jasmine into my muslin bag, pinned it again to my pillow, and cozied in for the night.

"Really?" Sedona said from the bottom of the bed. "You're doing the erotica thing *tonight*? Shouldn't you be concentrating on Esther and not your own disgusting human lust?"

"Oh, Sedona," I groaned. "You know me. It's not like this is the norm for me, right? It's been months since I've been with a man, even just for a coffee date! I have so much on my mind these days, things I can't control, human problems that just keep piling up. And today?" Suddenly I felt that throat knot again, threatening a cry jag.

I'm not a crier. I tend to store up all my problems that might be worth a few tears, and then I just let the dam break once in a blue moon. As in, I actually wait for the Blue Moon, which is about every two and a half years. On Blue Moon days, I take a ritualistic cleansing bath, then I have a very private opening ceremony where I bring forth the elements of Water from the West and Earth from the North. I say a quiet spell and light a black candle, black to absorb all the sadness and tears that have been building in me.

Then I commence to gather my tears. I literally gather them in a tiny vessel, throughout a marvelously long pity party for myself. Later, I use the tears for good. On my plants, of course.

It wasn't the Blue Moon tonight, but I felt a strange pull to cry.

"Oh, please," said Sedona. "So your ancient neighbor keeled over."

"You don't know that, do you?" I said. "What if someone

actually *killed* Ms. Esther? And besides, the whole Ms. Esther thing? That's a *fraction* of my problems. Just because I don't whine about my life all the livelong day doesn't mean I don't have *problems*, I'll have you know!"

"Yeah? Well cry me the Hudson River," Sedona said.

She's not normally nasty like this, I promise. Lately she had been locked out, locked in, neglected, abandoned, ignored, and, in her mind at least, starved. I swallowed and tried to put myself in her litterbox.

"Night, Sedona," I said, real soft and quiet so I wouldn't set her off and so I wouldn't get angry enough to get choked up again. I flicked off the light and scrunched up my pillow, taking a second to touch my Book of Shadows that rested next to my bed. My BOS held all of my magic: incantations, clever spells that rhymed perfectly, recipes for every imaginable problem and sadness and mystery the world could ever think to throw at me. Or my friends.

While I rolled the mystery earring around in my hand, I took a moment to be grateful for my friends, those still alive and those in or on their ways to Summerland. I didn't believe in Heaven and Hell but was very confident in the existence of a place that's warm and welcoming, somewhere just beyond our existence, where people who have passed from our world linger to meditate upon their next steps. Summerland, where my dad was, unless he'd chosen to move on by now, and where Ms. Esther would soon arrive, if she hadn't already.

Deep cleansing breath, a whisper to the Lord and the Lady, and soon I slept.

»>«<

Sure enough, my first picture is of a tiny naked troll doll with blue hair. He has those funny red cheeks and splayed nose and glass eyes that look like he's just up to some mischief. I ask him what his part is in all of this.

"Yeah, simple!" he says, "Yeah, I'm Hester Diamond's good luck charm. Once, she forgot me when she took one of those bus trips to Atlantic City. She lost a lot of money, see, and she's convinced the only way she can profit or at least break even is to have me in a prominent position at her table. Yeah, so she carries me in her purse on bingo days and I sit at her right hand through all of her games." He has a voice that reminds me of someone on Saturday Night Live, years ago. John Somebody with a snarky kind of tone, but as my mind is trying to place the guy, the troll starts to fade out. I focus, and the dream clears again.

"Do you know anything that would help in the case of Ms. Esther Sena's untimely death?" I ask him.

"Untimely? *Untimely*?" He falls over onto his back and dissolves in laughter. I stand and tap my foot with my arms crossed at my chest. "Okay, okay," he says, and stands up again. "Yeah, I do notice things, I mean my word, bingo can get boring, right?! And what I notice is this: Hester stares at your Esther's arm every bingo night, sometimes to the point where she misses the call, you know? Like, loses money because she's so obsessed with Esther's arm. One time? She cried. Yeah, she stared at that Esther's arm all through bingo, then she cried."

"Did Hester make it to bingo today?" I asked.

"It's not even 4:00 a.m., lady. No. No bingo yet today for anybody, thank the gods."

"Oh, yesterday, then. No, two days ago now, whew! Did she go to bingo two days ago?"

"Nope. Weird but true. Heard her on the phone saying she was having a blue day. Blue like my hair. Blue like your Blue Moon. Hester tells this person on the phone that she's blue. Yeah, she's staying home. That she can't bear to see all those old faces today. Some kind of anniversary or something."

"Wow," I say, even as I watch the troll pixilate and disappear.

»>«<

I didn't wake from that dream. I was aware that I was sleeping, but I was sure I could remember all that. Warning: Do not attempt this at home! You should always roust yourself up to record your dreams, especially if it's a critical dream like this one. I've had lots of experience, but I've learned that I'm sometimes a little over-confident when it comes to my memory.

»>«<

New scene, new dream: I am watching Miles from behind.

Now we're getting somewhere, I think.

He's carrying a bouquet of brilliant flowers, with sprays of exotic grasses jutting out from the bundle. My heart leaps, thinking maybe for some crazy reason the flowers are for me.

Miles is dressed impeccably, like he's ready to go out to dinner on some special occasion. He has a jacket on that is split right down the middle, half black, half camel. Like right where it buttons, half and half. Very strange but beautiful. Very John Legend. He's shifting his weight back and forth, in that cute little nervous habit I watched when he was right here, in my apartment.

He clears his throat, touches his breast pocket, takes a deep breath, then blows it into his fist to smell. He smiles. Such an incredible, full-faced smile that even while I know I'm sleeping, I still feel like I'm choking up.

He rings the doorbell, takes another breath.

No answer. He peers into the window on the side of the house, but the drapes have been pulled. We must be in the suburbs, or maybe a small town? There are sidewalks. Picket fences. The streetlights go on. I can't tell how much time has gone by.

Finally, Miles seems to make a decision. He reaches into the mailbox that hangs on the wall next to the front door, and dips his hand inside, fishing around a bit. He pulls out a key and bites the inside of his cheek as he stops to look at it, thinking. Then he puts it to the doorknob and steps inside.

My dream takes me with him. It is dark, so dark inside. Miles calls out, turns the corner into a living room, where candlelight greets him. I can feel his relief, his immediate excitement, as if someone has deliberately set this romantic stage for him. He smiles again.

But the smile is dashed when he realizes. He is horrified, embarrassed, then angry.

Then I understand what he's seeing. My eyes get used to the darkness, and they scan the room. The feathery flickering of the candle flames dance along the walls. Nine women are here, in the living room of the house. But the room is silent, like everyone is holding their collective breath. The air smells of incense.

I understand that they're all witches. It's a coven.

And all nine of them are skyclad.

They're all naked.

»>«<

I woke with a jolt, having almost felt Miles' palpable alarm for a moment. But after giving my hair a shake, I snorted a little bit in laughter and reached for my Book of Shadows. This, I couldn't afford to forget.

»>«<

I tossed and turned after that but must have gone into a twilight kind of sleep because I finally caught a glimpse of the earring I still held in my hand.

»>«<

It is brand new, the earring, but I can tell that my dream has brought me way back in time. I see finned cars in the streets, and the signs on the shops aren't neon. Women are wearing full-length fur coats, men are wearing fedoras. As if to help me in placing the timing, everything seems to be in sienna tones, dulled and faded. It's like an old movie.

Then the dream screen pans out, from the earring to its owner.

And there's Mrs. Peterson. Rita Peterson. Young and not at all bent over, she swings along the avenue like a magazine model, wearing a wide-brimmed hat and dark lipstick and a dress that cinches in at the waist then flares out. She is laughing, throwing her head back in silent hilarity, and she is arm in arm with—

"Harry," whispers the troll who is perched on my shoulder.

Chapter 26: Talk about our Dreams

The next afternoon, I sat in the shop, stirring a cup of tea and staring out at the street. Hannah had called and was on her way over as soon as she was finished with her regulars. A few of her customers have readings set up on a set schedule, just to check in to see if Hannah had heard any updates from their deceased. Sounds morbid, and it's a very expensive habit, but hey, everyone has their schtick, as Ms. Esther would say.

Used to say. I couldn't wrap my head around the reality of Ms. Esther being dead today, after just having held her hand in our séance last night. I stood up and took a huge stretch, clearing my mind of negativity, then started doing my rounds.

First, water. Always nice for some of my plant friends, to start a day with a nice refreshing drink. I watered the split-leaved philodendron, my mind teasing the dream memory of Esther's Phil and the earrings that might have fallen with him to the street. But probably didn't, leaving them for me to sell and living happily for a while after.

The herbs and florals, still in their winter slumber, were next on my nurture list, then the aloes and the snake plants and the ferns and the palms, some of them up to ten feet high. I straightened bags of dirt and tidied some dried arrangements and my mind was just starting to toy with the memory of watching Miles Denton from behind, when I heard my little front door bells.

Hannah looked kind of wrung out. Her eyes were red-rimmed and there were puffy bags under them. I put a fresh kettle on the stove for tea. Tea always helped.

"So?" I asked, taking a seat at the table. She plopped down across from me and rested her chin on her hands.

"Little crazy bug-eye staring through some kind of a portal," she said.

"Beg pardon?"

"Just one eye, staring through some kind of a microscope or telescope, that's what I dreamed. I'm talking almost all night, Maddie. Except for the one in the garden.

"In the second dream," she went on, "there were two girls holding hands, walking through a garden, maybe a park. Giggling, telling secrets. Their heads bent toward each other, hair blowing in the breeze. And a wind whispering, 'Esther, Hester,' over and over again. At one point, though? I'm seeing through a tube, maybe the same scope as before? Like maybe it's my eye in the first flash? Who knows. But I'm looking at Esther Sena's wrist. I'm seeing the silver bracelet from behind. There's a voice booming 'B31' and 'N20', and I suddenly see this old woman I've never laid eyes on before. She's staring at the silver bracelet, too. Then I'm looking through the tube again, and my eyes are on the lady I don't know, the one who's staring at Esther's bracelet. And then the dream dumps me back at the creepy eyeball. You?" She looked up with those sleepy eyes just as the kettle whistled and I jumped up to make a couple of cups of strong tea.

"Hmm. I have a troll with blue hair, just like you envisioned yesterday. Weird little guy, kind of a gangster personality. Seems he's Hester Diamond's good luck charm at the bingo games they all go to. Apparently, Hester missed bingo day before last. The day of the break-in. Called a friend and said she wasn't up for seeing all those people on account of it being an anniversary."

Hannah blew over her tea and one of her dreads dipped into it.

"Ew, Hannah," I said. I reached over to pull her hair out of the cup. She gave me a sleepy smile.

"Is that it? Just a troll who told you Hester called in sick for bingo?"

"No, there's another one." I hesitated, again because I still thought maybe the earrings could help me if things with Mother turned sour, but Hannah knew their story anyway, and Esther had, after all, told me they weren't hers, so I reached into my apron and put the earrings on the table between us.

"Last night I held one of these in my hand to give my dream magic an extra boost. And I dreamed of it in a black and white movie scene. Hannah, these belonged to Mrs. Peterson, the woman you saw in your shop vision yesterday. The one who's all bent over? Only in my dream, she was young and beautiful and sexy."

"Wow," Hannah said, looking more awake than she had before. "Does this mean…um. What does this mean? That Mrs. Peterson planted her earrings in a dying old plant in Esther's apartment? Why would she do such a thing?"

"But wait. There's more," I said. "In the dream, Mrs. Peterson was arm in arm with none other than Harry. Esther's Harry.

Dead Harry at the séance Harry." I looked at her over my mug, the steam warming my face.

We sat in silence for a while. I got up and locked the shop doors and turned the "Closed" sign over to the street.

"Might as well just hash it out, right?" said Hannah. "We have this triangle of women, one of them dead, and all three have had some sort of relationship with said dead woman's deceased husband."

"And lots of jewelry is floating around between them," I added. "Earrings from Phil's pot…they have to be from Phil's pot…not a pocket from just some passerby, right? Anyway, earrings show up with Mrs. Peterson and Harry. Bracelet shows up with Hester figuring prominently, seeing as dead Harry threw her under the bus at the séance. Plus, she shows up again in your garden dream with the girls, assuming they were Hester and Esther." I thought for a minute. "Plus don't forget she called in sick from bingo on the day the bracelet went missing…and then Sedona sees Mrs. Peterson bolting out of Ms. Esther's apartment last night, before she saw her, Ms. Esther, that is. Dead.

"And telescope eye?" Hannah asked. "What's up with that, do you think?"

"That's easy. That has to belong to creepy guy who lives across from Ms. Esther. Benson. Lloyd Benson. He spends hours of his day just standing 'watch' at his peep hole. Like a stalker, only a stationary stalker. Like a hunter in a stand."

"He has bugged out eyes?"

"Definitely. Bugged out."

Our spoons made musical little tinkling sounds together while we thought.

"Definite weirdness, between all of them," Hannah said. She

picked sleep out of one eyeball and inspected it. I let it go.

"They're all connected to this, you know," she went on. "There is no such thing as coincidence, no matter how much you believe in it, Maddie. And I don't care that they're all seniors. People don't just stop doing bad things to each other just because age has caught up with them. People are people."

"What, you think they're all in this together somehow? Like a gang? An octogenarian gang?" I thought about Harry. Was it possible that a dead guy, I mean a spirit, deliberately upset a member of the living in order to kill them?

"You think Harry's in on it?" I asked.

"You really are crazy, aren't you?" The voice was below me, and I watched Sedona swishing her fluffy gray tail from side to side. "Why don't you just butt out and let Dream Dude Denton solve this little mystery? Maybe get back to business, sell some plants, make some money, buy some salmon?"

I ignored her. "Maybe we should start at bingo." I took a sip of tea.

"Bingo," said Hannah and Sedona together.

"Yeah. Go to a bingo session, maybe that St. Joe's church that she would have gone to…" I looked at my wall calendar, a white board that I kept up to date on sales and events, things going on in the community. "…tonight, actually! Let's go watch a bingo game!"

They both just stared at me, so I kept going. "We deserve some fun, right? And they'll all be there! Or at least they could be. Benson, Peterson, Hester whatshername…Diamond, Hester's troll? They're all suspects, right?"

"Oh, definitely," Hannah said, but I knew she was turning snarky. "Because of evidence from a séance. And our dreams." She chewed on a blond dread.

I gave her the lifted lip.

"Hannah," I sniffed. "Okay, so maybe it's dumb. But you know what? I need a reset. There are too many ugly things going on. And bingo might just be fun. Plus maybe, just maybe..."

"Maybe what?"

"Maybe we could talk Officer Miles Denton into going with us? He could take his nephew! It'd be fun! A harmless little bingo game with a couple of merchants in his precinct just for the fun of it? Maybe we could even grab a bite to eat on the way home? What are the chances?" I gave her a hopeful grin.

"Slim to none," Sedona piped up from the floor. "Your dream bag is working overtime, my friend. Can a girl get a spot of cream here?"

"Yeah, yeah," I said, with a deflated sigh. I got up, poured some milk into her bowl and watched her while she lapped it up, all nice and dainty-like. "Okay, you're right. Probably no Miles Denton to accompany. But that's okay. He'd stick out like a sore thumb, anyway. Especially if he wore that uniform. But that doesn't mean we can't go there and sniff around a bit, right? You up for it?"

Hannah looked up at me and plucked her hair out of her mouth. "We're off to meet the troll, my friend."

Chapter 27: And into the Fire

We waited until almost six o'clock before we started walking. The day was fading, and the shadows had started to climb up the sides of the brownstones all around us.

"Should we get a cab?" I asked.

"Neh, we're young, it's not that far away, and we need the exercise, right?" Hannah stretched her arms up over her head and breathed in, yoga-style.

"Plus, these old people seem to be able to make it there okay," I said.

She laughed. "And they walk to all of these bingo places, right? From what you told me about Esther, not all of their games are at St. Joe's, right?" Hannah asked.

"Right. She mentioned this one at St. Joseph's as her favorite, but apparently there are all kinds of strange bingo sessions in bars these days, too, not just churches. Drag queen clubs, non-profits, animal rescues, you name it, there's a bingo game going on somewhere. It's like the new AA." We laughed together and linked arms.

"What if this isn't the right one, then?"

"I'm pretty sure I heard her right the other day. Gosh, two days ago! Is it really only Wednesday? Can you believe we were all getting ready for the séance with good old Harry just yesterday, just about this time of day? And now, she's just gone?! Crazy." We walked in silence for a while, both of us watching people and dogs and traffic.

"And back to your question, I don't think we care if any of our suspects are at this game, anyway, right?" I asked. "We just want to see it in action, watch for trolls, watch the people, see if they're hooking up or going out together afterward. You know, detective work. Plus fun. Never forget fun."

St. Joseph's Catholic Church looks more like a public library than a church, set proudly on the corner of Sixth Street and Washington Place. We stopped in front of it before climbing the stairs and collected ourselves.

"Do you have any money?" Hannah asked in a sing song voice.

"Gotcha covered, girlfriend, no problem. This is a favor you're doing for me, right?" I dug through the carpetbag. It took a while, with several hand-offs to Hannah of various items for me to locate my wallet.

We followed signs to get to where the bingo action was, down the stairs and into the bowels of the building. We could hear the chatter of people at the game already in session, and finally we stood before a fold-out table with two ladies perched behind it. A metal firebox full of bills was between them.

"Minimum of three cards, Dear," said one of them. She smiled up at us through squinted eyes as if she'd forgotten to wear her glasses, but she hadn't. I handed over a twenty and hoped she could see what it was, and I was relieved when her friend scooped in for my money.

"We'll set you up with three cards each, then? Or are you here for the evening?" We looked at her with what must have been obvious ignorance, and they shared a wise look between them. "You beginners?"

"Oh, yes, and you know, we're really here just to watch," I said.

"Can't."

"Can't?"

"Can't just watch," she said, enunciating each word as if I might be hard of hearing.

"Oh, that's fine. That's why I'm paying, see?" I pointed at my twenty.

They worked it out okay, but I was starting to understand that maybe Ms. Esther and Mrs. Peterson and all their friends just liked to be around people their own age, that maybe it wasn't so much the game as it was the community, elderly folks all playing together and chatting each other up with the help of their hearing aids and their magnifying glasses and their trolls.

We were interlopers, Hannah and I, and I sensed their suspicion.

As the ladies argued over my change and openly eyed us up and down, Hannah stifled her giggles. It reminded me of church laughter with my best friend when I was little. In the silence of the prayer, we would try so hard to not laugh that we would laugh even harder, but we would plug up our noses to keep it in, so that when it finally came out it was in a series of snorts, which made us laugh even harder. Mother would stab me in my thigh with her sharp fingernails, and that would make us start all over again.

I blinked away the thought of my mother and ushered

Hannah past the nice welcoming ladies. With our cards in hand, we found ourselves a couple of seats toward the back of the hall.

Finally, Hannah and I were launched into our very first, and maybe, probably, our last, bingo game.

Blue hair surrounded us, and not just from the folks who were busy punching their daubers onto their bingo cards as the guy up front shouted out letters and numbers.

The blue hair was also on trolls. Trolls were everywhere, perched on the tables, their round vacuous eyeballs peeking out of purses, even pinned into some woman's bun at the top of her head. Blue hair, pink hair, brilliant banana hair, everywhere.

Hannah and I leaned into each other. We didn't need to suppress our church laughter here.

"We aren't really going to play these games, are we?" Hannah asked, fanning her laughter away with her three bingo cards.

"Well, sure! Why the heck not? Fun, remember?" I said. "What if we were to win lots of money? Maybe pay your rent with the winnings?" I shrugged off my coat and plunked down my carpetbag, scanning the crowd. "Keep your eye open for Hester. Or Mrs. Peterson. Woman of your dreams." We giggled. "Oh, or Mr. Benson, telescope man."

Hannah spit a dreadlock out of her mouth. "You think he's the murderer?"

"We don't even know for sure if Ms. Esther was murdered yet, Hannah," I said, getting a good look at the dauber they'd given me at the doorway. It was just a little ink stamp like we used to play with when we were kids. I wondered if you had to lick it to keep it working.

"Well what, then?"

"Hmm?" I said. "No" was the answer to the licking question.

The taste of ink from the dauber made me look around frantically for something to drink.

"What's the eyeball mean?"

"Oh, I think maybe he knows something, and he hasn't told Miles yet. Or maybe he saw what happened, like he saw who came to Ms. Esther's apartment." I grabbed a napkin out of my bag and licked it to get that ink off. Awful.

"Besides Mrs. Peterson, you mean? Because we already know that."

"Shh! Isn't that Mr. Google Eye's little bald head up there?" I tried to point with my elbow, so I wouldn't look rude. Mother always said, "Don't point!"

"I wouldn't know Mr. Benson if he fell out of my back-hall closet," Hannah said. "You'll have to walk up there to check him out."

"No, I'll just bide my time. Ooh, that lady just screamed Bingo! That means we can start. Put all your cards out in front of you. Here," I said, and I pulled out two crystals. One was a peridot, green and faceted almost like a diamond, and the other one was just my tourmaline quartz that I carried for power. I gave the peridot to Hannah and she touched it in awe.

"Wha?! I think my heart stopped a little just now." She picked it up and massaged it between her thumb and index finger. "Where did you get this? These are pretty hard to find, Maddie!" She looked up at me in wonder. "These are supposed to bring great fortune!"

"Truth? I think I picked it up at a Wicca kiosk at a West Virginia beer fest a couple of years ago."

"Well, and look at you now," she said.

"Hannah. My dad *died.* That's not exactly what I'd call financial luck." I rolled my eyes again, but I could tell she felt flustered that it had come out of her mouth sounding like that.

"I'm sorry," she said.

"Shh. They're starting!" I clutched my quartz and sent up a quick prayer to Hades, god of wealth and lots of other things.

It was all very exciting, really. I can see how this whole scene might become addicting, because they get you so you're almost there, little dauber dots all in a row up or down or diagonally, and you're sure you're going to win--sometimes up to a thousand dollars--but then wham! Someone else screams out "Bingo!" And you have to start all over again.

In the middle of the second game, I slid my cards over to Hanna. I wanted to sleuth. Staring at the back of that little bald head, I was positive it was him, Mr. Benson, but I'd need to walk up and see his face to be sure.

I excused myself and slid out to where they had a big thermos of coffee in the back of the room. I poured myself a cup. I'm not usually a coffee woman, but that dauber inky taste was still sitting on my tongue.

"B 38?" the guy at the front called, his voice going up at the end like he was asking a question. Then again, "B 38," only this time it was a definite sentence. He looked proud to be the voice of power tonight, and I wondered if it was always him, or if they took turns, or drew names out of a hat.

Dad used to laugh at all the things I wondered about. Once in a while he would carry a little clicker in his pocket and click it every time I said the word "wonder."

"I wonder where that little clicker is now," I wondered out loud, then held my hand in front of my mouth. No one seemed to hear me, though.

I listened to the man as he pulled the little balls out of the bingo popper, just like they do for the state lottery on television right before Jeopardy comes on. Slowly, trying to look like a woman just stretching her legs, I made my way past our row until I could see the bald guy's profile.

Sure enough, Mr. Lloyd Benson.

I shrank back to my seat and looked at Hannah's cards. "Hey, you're almost there!" I said, and she shushed me.

"Don't jinx me!"

"Right, sorry." I looked up at Mr. Benson. He seemed stilted, almost frozen in place, and he wasn't bent over his bingo cards like everybody else. Instead, he stared off to his left.

I followed the line of his gaze, through the row of people in front of him, and my eyes finally landed on a woman with gray hair (which, let's face it, almost everyone had), but who now excitedly waved a bingo card over her head, and screamed, "Bingo!"

Mr. Benson's head tilted upward as if to look at the winning card, and I could tell he was smiling just from the angle of his face and muscles in the back of his stretchy little turtle neck.

My eyes followed his gaze up, up the length of her arm, where a beautiful and faintly familiar looking bracelet now rested.

It shone and sparkled under the fluorescent lighting. Just a simple silver band, with little diamonds encrusted along its rims. I felt the goosebumps travel up my spine.

We waited until they took a break, just like a little intermission before another round, and then Hannah and I scurried to the exit to catch Mr. Benson as he made his way to the bathroom.

"Mr. Benson!" I shouted over the bingo fan chatter. He had the braceleted woman by the arm and was leading her toward us with a satisfied little smile on his chicken lips. I took advantage of the jostling of the crowd to get another good look at the bracelet.

I'd filled Hannah in by then and told her to just let me do the talking.

"Hello!" I said, all cheery and excited. "We decided to check out what all the fuss is about, and Hannah almost won, but hey!" I looked at the woman and stuck out my hand. "Looks like you beat her to it! Congrats!"

The woman was flushed and put her pudgy hand in mine, smiling through gray teeth.

"Oh, thank you! I can't remember the last time I won anything! And this one was a *thousand* dollars, if you can even *imagine*!" She pulled her hand away from mine and held it to her chest. "I hope I don't have a heart attack over it!" She laughed, and it was like the sound of angels laughing, musical and trickling down the scale until it ended in a little cough.

"Well congratulations again, er..."

"Oh!" said Mr. Benson, "Where are my manners? Let me introduce you. Miss Bridges, am I right? Meet my dear friend, Hester. Hester Diamond."

Chapter 28: Meet Me at the Station

Well, Hannah and I couldn't wait to get out on the street after meeting Hester Diamond.

"Hester Diamond has Ms. Esther's bracelet on!" I said. "It matches the description she gave the police perfectly! Just a simple silver band, with little diamonds encrusted all along the rims!"

"So wait," Hanna said. "We're saying that Hester Diamond stole the bracelet from Esther? Like broke into her apartment?" Does that even make sense? Do old ladies break into other old ladies' apartments to take jewelry?"

She had a point, there.

"Maybe Hester has a key just like Mr. Benson and Mrs. Peterson. Seems like Ms. Esther trusted a lot of people with her apartment."

"Or was really paranoid that she'd die alone in there and no one would come to check on her until she started to smell."

"Ew, Hannah!" I stopped dead in my tracks. We had started walking toward home, and now were at the corner of 10th and Hudson. "Let's turn here, stop in at the police station real quick."

"Really? And what, might I ask, are we going to turn in as our newly-found evidence? We saw a bracelet, Maddie." Hannah said, catching her breath.

"How many bracelets in this world match that particular description, huh?" I had stopped dead in my tracks. "'Just a simple silver band, with little diamonds encrusted along its rims,' that's how she described it, and that's what we saw. On the arm of the woman who was its original owner, yet! We're going to march to Officer Miles Denton, and we're going to tell him what we've seen, and then we're going to let him fend for himself. Meanwhile, I'm going to get to work on getting a first-hand witness' account of the theft."

"Meaning?"

"I think," I said, "it's time for my magic touch, my friend. At the humble abode of a certain Mr. Lloyd Benson."

»>«<

We didn't exactly "march" to the police station, but we did get there, and were told that Officer Denton was indeed still here and would see us in a few minutes. I wondered where.

"You think maybe in one of those rooms like you see on television, where they take the criminals to interrogate them? And the whole time there are detectives watching from behind the glass?"

"Maybe, sure," Hannah said. She looked tired.

I dug around in my carpetbag and pulled out half a lemon, tucked neatly into a plastic bag, and a rewrapped piece of sugarless peppermint candy that I may have and may not have already sucked on once.

Hannah lifted her lip. "Ew, Maddie. Is this candy *used*?"

I laughed. "Oh, so what. Any woman who sucks on her own hair can't have too much to say about her best friend's second-hand candy. Here." I pierced the lemon's rind with my fingernail and twisted it, then held it up to Hannah's nose. She smiled almost immediately.

"See? Citrus makes us feel sunny," I said. "It rejuvenates the spirit. Now pop this in." I pressed the candy between her lips just as Miles Denton came through the doors to the waiting area. He stood watching us as I finished my magic au naturel. "The peppermint has natural properties that help wake up the mind and refresh the senses." I smiled at her, then up at Miles.

"Officer Denton, good to see you again." I shook his hand, but used both of mine, enveloping his and diving into his eyes. I could feel my energy renew just looking at him, all fresh in his nice clean uniform.

"Ms…Maddie," he said, and he extended the hand that I reluctantly released toward Hannah. "Hannah? What brings you two here this evening?"

"Aren't we going to meet in a secluded beige room with one-way mirrors?" I asked, peeking over his shoulder.

"Not unless you have confidential information you'd rather not have any other constituents hearing," he said, flashing me those teeth.

"Oh, I'm pretty sure this would be considered confidential, yes. Definitely important evidential information, Officer."

He looked down at me and finally shrugged. "Well, welcome, then. Let's see if we can find someplace more private."

We followed him into the station, and he wound around desks and people as if he'd been working there for years. After tapping on a door that was cracked open, he pushed on it and stuck his head in, then stepped into a room.

It was sort of like the television rooms, kind of yellow and bland, with cups on the window sills. The floor was sticky. We sat down, with me across from him and Hannah next to me. I pulled my chair in and deliberately touched his shoe with mine, then left it there, trying to hide the flush of triumph that rose to my face.

"We found the bracelet, Miles. We went to bingo and there it was on Hester Diamond's arm!" I said in a flood of words that seemed to burst from me like the spray from a fire hose.

Miles leaned back in his chair with his beautiful muscled arms crossed in front of him and put his pencil between his lips.

"Pretty sure that proves she's the thief," Hannah piped in. "Or at least she has something to do with Esther's case. Plus, we both put our dream bags under our pillows last night, and one of my dreams was Hester and Esther together as schoolgirls, giggling with their heads together. Then in my other dream, I saw this goofy eyeball through like a telescope? Maddie figured out that was Esther's neighbor, Lloyd Benson, who stands at his door all day and spies out his peephole."

"Plus," I interrupted, because honestly, Hannah just loves center stage too much, "I had a troll dream, just like the one who came to Hannah at the séance, so, we went to bingo to research trolls, and sure enough--"

"Ladies, ladies," Miles said, not moving a muscle. He was smiling, but I got the distinct feeling the words that he was preparing in his head right now were not going to be pleasant for Hannah and me to hear.

"You know as well as I do that I can't go to my sergeant with dreams and séance visitors, right?" He stood up as if that was that and we were all done. I stayed very firmly put in my sticky chair.

"We know that, Miles. We just thought you should have all the pieces of the puzzle, even if some of them were found using magic. You're probably smart enough to find a way to move around the magic and find out who's behind this whole thing." I looked with a critical eye at my cuticles. I should get down to the *Nailed It*! salon soon.

"Unless," I continued, "you'd rather us just butt out. Which is fine with us. We both have businesses to run, lives to live..."

"I didn't mean to offend," he said. We locked eyes for just a spit of a moment. "It's just that the preliminary results from the Coroner's office do confirm that Esther Sena died of a cardiac arrest, which is not uncommon in people of her age, and I have a couple of other cases that are really pressing right now. I didn't mean to be short with you."

I could almost see his brain wheels chinking as I watched his eyes fall on my hand. He wanted to touch it.

I sat up straighter, caught his eye, and tried to give him a gracious smile. "Sure. No, we get it. We just were stopping off on the way, anyway. Sorry to bother. Come on, Hannah," I said as we stood and got our things together. Hannah still had one of her bingo cards clutched in her hand.

"There are more dreams you haven't heard, yet, Miles. Mrs. Peterson dreams, strange musical chairs games with pieces of jewelry...we'd be happy to tell you about them." I had my hand on the doorknob. "And we'd love to hear what *your* dreams were last night, too. Did you put the bag under your pillow?"

He let his head fall down until his chin rested on his neck and smiled to himself.

"Ooh! You did!" I laughed a little. "Come over some time! Or call me. We can tell each other our dreams later?"

I know I was starting to blush and blather and Hannah knew it, too. She took me by the elbow and led me back out through all the desks.

"Thanks again, Officer," she said to him as he walked behind us to the waiting area.

Which is where we found Mrs. Rita Peterson, hunched over herself and crying.

Chapter 29: The Dragon's Lair

Of course I wanted to stay. I wanted to conjure up a spell and get Mrs. Peterson all to myself so I could figure out her part in all of this. But Miles gave me a stern look, then flashed a look at the officer behind the front desk, a new guy, not that Officer McCartony guy, then looked back at me. I didn't want to make him look bad on the job.

So we left.

"I get the exact word 'confession' from just looking at her, Maddie," said Hannah as soon as the big glass door had swung shut behind us.

"Really?"

"Really. That's why she was such a mess in there! She going to confess to the murder!"

"Hannah, we just heard from Miles who heard from the Coroner that Ms. Esther died naturally."

"'Preliminary findings' is what he said, Maddie. I'm telling you, I heard her, saw right through her, like she was made of transparent glass. She had the word 'confession' ready to spill out of her mouth the second Miles gets her alone."

"Hey!" I had that lightbulb thing happen. "Maybe she's going to confess to something else? Like breaking and entering. She did that, last night, after all."

"Like as much as you did," Hannah said. "She has a key, remember? It's not breaking and entering if you were given a key."

"Well, she's old. Maybe she's just confused." We were at the corner of Bleeker and 10th; it was time to part ways. "I'll call you," I said. "And thank you, Hannah. Thanks for everything you are." We hugged, and I walked toward home, grateful for my magical best friend.

I opened the shop just long enough to get the mail and do a quick check on my babies. A flash of insight struck as I passed the oils and herbs display on the side wall, and I ran my fingers along the bottles until they landed on the Louisiana Swamp Serum. I smiled. Magic time, indeed. This would be perfect.

Then it was up to my apartment to get my act together for my Lloyd Benson Q & A. Sedona looked up from the couch when I walked in, then let her eyes close again. I didn't want to stir her up, so I just tiptoed to my room.

The earrings from the sidewalk were lying on my dresser, and I put them on my ears carefully, biting my tongue as I watched myself in the mirror. They were simple pearls, set into silver clasps that screwed onto my lobes. Small enough to not call attention to themselves, they still looked beautiful on me, their clusters of diamonds surrounding the pearls like constellations. Kind of out of my wheelhouse of feathers and big hoops, but maybe nice for a date, when I might want to go a little more conservative.

"Nice," I said softly, still careful not to wake up the princess.

Who knew? Maybe I'd go on a date this spring. Maybe I'd get to stop into Bravo a Cuore after all. Stranger things had happened. I tipped my Swamp Serum up and dabbed just a drop on each ear, sort of like Mother used to do as I watched her get ready to go out. I shrugged that memory away and dabbed another drop onto my palms, which I rubbed together. Another quick dab on the wrists, and I was set.

I smiled at my reflection and set off for Lloyd Benson's spy stand.

It occurred to me that fear might be a healthy wing woman in this little field trip, just to keep me cautious. Benson could, after all, be the thief. Or the killer. Or even both. So what if he was old and I could probably push him over with my index finger? I still needed to be careful.

What if he poisoned people? What if the creepy feeling I got from him was because he actually *was* a creeper? Like what if he was perverted or had some kind of morbid collection? Like eyeballs? Or tongues? What if he locked me in his apartment like a spider in his web, and held me there until I died?

I was getting all worked up, so I turned back, went into the store again, and grabbed my bottle of Caution, which I'd mixed myself. For myself. It's a mixture of the sappy stuff from the roots of a plant only found north of the Tropic of Cancer, the Rhodiola rosea. I had added to that the crushed dried leaves of some New York City Gingko trees and a few choice Sumatran coffee beans.

Taken with a cup of tea, just a half a teaspoon, this concoction works to make me extremely focused, with a healthy edge of fear, and no possibility of distraction. Whatever Lloyd Benson's sneaky or perverted ways, I would be ready for him, index finger locked and loaded.

I was on tiptoe, still smacking my lips from my Caution tea, but definitely focused by the time I got to the second floor.

He was there when I reached his apartment; I could feel it, his creepy energy radiating through the door. I tried to avert my eyes from Ms. Esther's door as I lifted my fist to knock on Mr. Benson's.

No need. He had been there and was waiting, just as I'd thought. His skinny little face peeked out of the crack in his door. His chain lock was still latched.

"Hello, good evening, yes," he said, and it confused me, all those random things at once, but I collected myself and raised my hand in hello.

"Mr. Benson, I just wanted to drop in to see how you were faring. I know this whole business with Ms. Esther, first the robbery and now her death, must be weighing on you. Being not only a neighbor but a friend. Well, a friend who also is a Co-Bingo....er." I didn't know what to call her, so what the heck. "Awfully nice, meeting your other bingo friend this evening," I added.

He looked up at my raised hand and his eyes latched onto my ring. I smiled despite the strange vibe.

"I'm wondering if you might have a minute just to chat? You live so close to her that I--"

"Are you a police officer now?" Mr. Benson interjected. "Because your buddy and I already had this conversation today, and I don't really feel like reiterating the whole schlemiel again. Maybe you two got your wires crossed." He stared out the five-inch opening, and I got the definite feeling that was as wide as he wanted his door to open tonight.

"Jeez, Mr. Benson," I said, looking down at his shoes. Old, but nicely shined. "No, of course I'm not a police officer. You know that. I'm the owner of *The Garden Witch,* where you bought an Amaryllis bulb for your daughter at Thanksgiving.

I'm the one you came to when your friendship plant's leaves went all soft and shriveled. Remember? You know me." I looked up and batted my eyelashes at him, just once. And for extra effect, I licked my lips. I lowered my hand and touched the ring lovingly with my other hand.

That must have been the secret code for Mr. Lloyd Benson, because wow, suddenly he couldn't wait to get me inside. He slammed the door and I could hear him messing with the chain, and then poof! Like magic, I was inside. I was careful to put out my hand right away.

I took his hand in mine, and with both of my hands, gave his palm a good once-over while searching his face and hoping my expression showed a measure of concern. I felt the heat from the truth serum smear from my palms to his, and I made sure my wrists were facing up so that he could breathe it in as well as absorb it.

"Thank you, Mr. Benson."

"Lloyd, please. Call me Lloyd." His thin little lips cracked as he smiled at me, then down at our hands. "Have a seat!" he said, waving. "Anywhere! Can I get you a drink?"

Wow, I thought, I'm royalty, and all it took was the old eyelash-lip-ring combo? "No, thanks. I'm good." I sat on an overstuffed couch that was covered in plastic and crinkled with resistance as it took my weight. "Really, I just wanted to see how you were, Mr., um, Lloyd."

"Oh, I'm just fine. You know, Miss..."

"Maddie, call me Maddie."

"Ah, Maddie. Cute. I knew a Labradoodle named Maddie once. Anyway, Maddie. We old people know we're going to check out of here sooner or later. Esther and I walked to bingo together, but we weren't really all that close." I caught his eyes dart to the right, then, as if he were checking himself.

"You know, I might just have to change my mind about that drink, Lloyd," I said. "Just a glass of water, maybe? It's been a heck of a week, and I haven't been drinking enough water."

"Ah, well, who does, these days?" he said as he rose. "Have you heard how much they're saying we should be drinking? My word, I would just float away if I drank what they want me to!" He gave a weird little laugh and shuffled his way into the kitchen.

While he was in there, I checked out what he had looked at while he was talking to me. I stood up, pretended to look at the horse and hound painting over his marble table, then let my gaze fall down to the table's surface.

And there, in a deep and shining mother-of-pearl bowl, was a pile of jewelry.

Women's jewelry.

Chapter 30: Inside Information

When I finally wrenched my eyes away from all that jewelry, Mr. Benson was coming out of the kitchen with my glass of water. My heart did a flip or two as he casually flipped a third lock on his door.

He slinked over to me, bent down to place my glass on a coaster, and joined me at the mother-of-pearl bowl.

"Pretty, isn't it?" he whispered. "Silver just does it for me. He gazed up at me and his eyes ran all over my face and my body.

Pretty creepy, I thought.

"Um. Yes, very pretty," I said. I touched each ear and rubbed my palms together while desperately thinking of something to say that wouldn't end up getting me robbed. Or killed. I looked back at the jewelry, then back at him. I held my tongue.

"I collect," he said with a tight-lipped smile.

"It would appear that way, yes," I said, reaching for my glass.

"I collect from the women who visit me," he said. His eyes were glazing over as if he were starting to fall asleep, and I steered him gently toward the couch. I knew the truth serum was starting to do its job. I patted my pockets and found my phone.

I tapped a few icons to start the voice recording like Hannah had taught me, very high-tech of me if I do say so myself, then put it upside down on the coffee table. I pretended to take a sip of water and kept my voice really soothing for my first, and, judging from every television drama I've ever watched, my most important question.

"You're okay if we record our talk, yes, Mr. Benson?"

"Yes," he said, smiling.

"So, you collect jewelry from women, Mr. Benson?"

"Lloyd. Please."

"Sure. Lloyd. What women visit you here?"

"You'd be surprised, Miss Madeline. You'd be surprised."

"Try me." I leaned toward him, rapt in attention, but also focused on Benson's body. Could I really take him down if I had to? He didn't look like a murderer, all spindly and skinny limbs, crooked posture, and rheumy bug eyes. Could I even imagine this creaky old man murdering Ms. Esther?

"Well. You young folks seem to think that all love dies on the vine when we age. My children, they don't even believe the stories of my love affairs. They look at me like I've got feathers coming out my ears." He clasped his gnarled fingers together and I looked down at his spotted hands.

"But I'm here to tell you," he went on, "that love is alive and well in folks as old as me, and I'm a living testimony to it. There's a pill for everything these days. Did you know," he said, with a mischievous sparkle in his eyes, "that venereal disease is more prevalent in assisted living facilities than it is in college dormitories?" He let a bark of a phlegmy laugh escape his lips and I pulled back.

"Well no, I did not know that one. No," I said, horrified. Never comfortable talking about sex, this was edging toward a line I'd have to draw fairly soon.

"Sure, sure. The ladies who live on this block? The ladies who play bingo? Heck, even some of those prudes at church? They're all hot to trot, if you know what I mean." He winked at me and I tried to make my grimace turn into a pleasant smile. "Frankly, I thought maybe that was why you might be stopping in today yourself!" He patted me on the leg and I stopped breathing. "Word does have a way of getting around, you know."

"Oh gosh." I stood, straightened my muumuu and started backing up toward the door, but then I remembered the phone. As I leaned down to get it, Mr. Benson stood up and his lips were on my cheek faster than lightning.

"Mr. *Benson*!" I shouted, and if Ms. Esther had still been alive, she would have heard me all the way over in her bedroom. Why in Hades' name hadn't I told Hannah to call me in the middle of this meeting? Why hadn't I at least woken up Sedona and told her to keep a ledge lookout just in case I ended up like poor Ms. Esther?

Oh. Ms. Esther. I had to stay, I realized. I had to get a grip, trust my magic and my strength. I had to play this thing out to get my information. I looked at him and smiled, but kept my distance, my phone safely in hand. I could always call 911.

"I admire your earrings," he said. "I could swear I'd seen them before." He shuffled over to me and blinked as he examined them. His eyes were by now watery, his gaze far away. He squinted to focus. "Beautiful little pearls. Pearls encased in silver. And vintage!" He whistled soft and secretively.

Then his eyes went wide, and his lips closed and opened. I thought of my childhood pet goldfish for the second time this week. "Rita! Rita Peterson had earrings just exactly like that!

She was just here a few days ago! And then--" He stopped himself short. "Uh, beautiful woman, Rita."

Again, his eyes glazed over, and I prayed to Athena for strength and wisdom.

"She left them here, of course. Just like they all end up leaving their pieces here. I make sure of that." He smiled up at me like an innocent kid selling lemonade on the street for five bucks a cup.

"You make sure of it? How's that?" I asked.

"Well, it's just the very best thing you can give to a woman, jewelry," he said. "Best thing to get, too."

"I'm not following."

"I allow them to leave pieces here, let's say I move the nicer pieces when the ladies are…shall we say…indisposed?" He winked again. "And they forget all about those pieces because some of them leave here with a new piece, and maybe…shall we say…a piece of me, too?"

"I get it," I said, putting my hands up so he'd know to stop, stop, stop putting visions of octogenarian naked ladies in my head. "But I'm not following the *why* of it all, Mr. Benson. Lloyd," I corrected myself before he could intervene.

"By the time you get to eighty," he said, settling back down on the couch, "it's easy to start thinking that nothing is going to change in life anymore. It's all one big routine, and for the most part, you appreciate that. You eat, you shop, you play a game or two with friends, you eat again, you nap, you eat again, you watch television, you go to bed. Same circle every day."

He stopped to take a drink of my water, and I know I saw some of his sip wash back into the glass. I shuddered.

"I like to be the agent of change." He stood up and gave

a feeble pounding to his chest. "I *am* the *Agent of Change*! That's what I tell them. It makes them laugh. Some of them cry, they laugh so hard. It's easy, to make an old lady's day, Maddie Bridges." He found a tissue in his breast pocket and half-heartedly wiped at his pointy nose.

"And as the Agent of Change…you do what?" I was hesitant to ask that one. Please no sex positions, please no sex toy talk, I prayed.

"I take them to interesting places. Not far away, just shops they might never have visited, restaurants a couple of blocks away, sometimes even a tavern. I tell them how lovely they are. Not a woman alive, I don't care what your age, who doesn't need to hear that once in a while."

He dabbed at one of his eyes. "And…I give them jewelry. Jewelry that I got somewhere else. That's all. It makes them swoon. Well, as long as they don't realize I've moved the jewelry they wore in here. That's where it gets a little sticky." He chuckled. "Most of them assume they've just misplaced their piece at home, maybe even forgot to wear it when they came here to visit. I play dumb, tell them I didn't think they were wearing any jewelry when they walked in my door."

He closed his eyes and for a moment I thought maybe the serum had put the poor guy to sleep. But then the tongue wormed its way out and the eyes pried open. He gave me sort of a conspiratorial smile. "It's just that lately a little bit of the romance has been, shall we say, costly?"

"Costly?"

"Yes, lately, they've been catching on, I think. Don't get me wrong, it's still wildly exciting, but, well…"

"…were you Ms. Esther's *Agent of Change,* Mr. Bens--Lloyd?"

"Hmm? Oh, gosh, no. Esther Sena is most definitely not my type! Ha! Haha! That's rich." He dabbed his eyes. "But yes, you could say I fumbled the ball just a bit with her."

"Mr. Benson?" I leaned in and touched his knee. "Did you borrow Ms. Esther's bracelet? The simple silver band with little diamonds encrusted along its rims?"

"Oh, please don't tell the nice police officer that, Maddie!" He looked at me and his eyes started to water again. "I'm not a thief!" He stood and started pacing with a definite limp in his gait.

"Look, Lloyd," I said, turning my phone over to make sure the recorder was still going. "I'm sure there's a really good and well-intentioned story behind it, but if you can lend any insight to this case at all, we'd be helping our police force get on with what might be, uh, things that might be more pressing in our neighborhood."

He clutched at his neck and started crying in earnest, his feeble shoulders heaving with his sobs.

I felt like such an awful person, coming in here and making an old man weep. I stood and put my arms around him.

"I'm sure," I said, "that since you're Ms. Esther's friend and neighbor, and since she had given you a key to her apartment, that this can all be explained very easily, Mr. Benson. It just seems like a bigger deal because--"

"Because she *died!*" he wailed. "This is all my fault!"

I let the silence sit, because sometimes that's what it takes. He seemed to be collecting his words, his eyes wild and his lips stretched out in a grimace.

"I told a lie to Rita," he whispered.

"Rita? Oh, Mrs. Peterson?"

"Yes. I told her I'd seen her earrings on Esther Sena just the other day. I don't know what made me lie, Maddie. Please, I'm not a bad man, and I know this sounds–"

"It's okay, Lloyd. Just breathe. I'm right here." I touched his hand again, hoping enough of the serum was still left.

"She went storming off…she has a key to Esther's place, you know. Ha! I guess we all do!" His hands fluttered around his face, and finally rested there for a moment. I counted to three.

"And I'm just surmising, here, but when Rita got into Esther's bedroom, I think that's when Esther had her…her…heart attack!"

"But why, Lloyd? Why would you tell Rita that Esther might have her earrings in the first place?"

"Well." His eyelids were veined, almost transparent. "I felt awful about borrowing Esther's beautiful bracelet. But Hester, I call her *my* Hester," and here he gave a bashful little grin, "My Hester has been talking about that bracelet as long as I've known her. Said she would stare at Esther Sena's wrist and feel her heart breaking, just like she was a young girl again. Seems the bracelet, and if you ask me, it's not even that pretty, seems it had originally belonged to Hester, anyway. Really, I was almost justified. But I did feel guilty, Maddie, believe me. So I…I swapped her. When I borrowed the bracelet, I took Rita's earrings over there and kind of tucked them in."

"Into one of her plants?" I asked.

"Well, not exactly. Damn thing was packed in dirt that felt like concrete! So I just slipped them under the plant, that little hole all those pots have, you know. But wait!" He blinked. "How on earth could you have known about the plant?

Chapter 31: Truth Hurts

After I'd settled him down, gotten him a cup of tea, and soothed him with a peace spell, my head was spinning. I knew that I finally had a crucial and non-magical piece of evidence. Well, non-magical except for the Louisiana Swamp Serum I'd smeared all over his hands in order to get it. I knew I should get my phone straight to the police station.

I called Hannah instead.

We met at the corner then hustled down to the station, me gripping my phone instead of tossing it into my carpetbag like usual. When we got there, though, the officer at the front desk, that guy who reminded me of a toad, Officer McCartony, told us that Miles Denton was in a meeting and might be a while. He sure worked a lot, I thought idly, though I guess I usually do, too.

Worked a lot, I mean. (By now, the Caution concoction was wearing off, and I was slowly regaining my old distracted self.)

"So?" Hannah said, after we took our coats off and made ourselves at home in the waiting area, "You still haven't told me about your Mother of a Meeting. Your Maternal Madness. Your Uptown Upset." She raised an eyebrow at my expression.

"Too soon?"

"No, I just don't know if we need to go there here. I mean, talk about that, here," I said. "It's sad and complicated, Hannah." I looked up at McCartony, busying himself with paperwork at his desk, and not minding us one bit. Still, I hesitated to discuss my private life at all, let alone in a public place.

Hannah shrugged. "Just cast one of those quiet spells. You can do that, right? Use it or lose it, my friend."

She was right. I tended to hold back on my magic unless it was absolutely necessary. This seemed like kind of a selfish use of it, but I was exhausted from the last few days and hadn't had enough time to sort through my own drama while this jewelry heist had been brewing.

I nodded my head as I found my bag of lavender. I grabbed a pinch of it, sprinkled a little into Hannah's open hand, and kept the rest. Then I whispered my spell:

Let our voices not be heard,
Make their ears hear not a word.
Give us space and time to share
Matters placed in private care.

"I think she hates me, Hannah."

"No, that's not possible. Mothers can't hate their kids. Pfft!"

"And furthermore," I went on, "I think I hate her right back."

"No, Maddie! Don't even send that kind of thought out into the Universe! This is just a character-building time, that's all. For both of you." She saw my exasperated expression and reached out to touch my face. "She needs to see that money isn't the only thing that could disappear because of her actions. And you?" She grabbed a dreadlock and chomped on it. "You need to learn how to forgive and move on."

I looked around, and sure enough, Officer McCartony was on the phone, not even registering that we were speaking. A man who had come into the station stood by the desk, tapping his toe and waiting to talk with McCartony, but not even turning to notice us. It was like we were invisible.

"I offered to pay the taxes on the house. But that's all. This time. Part of me just wants to hand over all the money and just let her go, Hannah. But that's not what Dad wanted. And after hearing about what she's been doing, apparently for years, it's not what I want, either."

Hannah touched my shoulder and closed her eyes. "I can't hear your dad here, but I feel him, Maddie. Dead or no, we never stop learning, my friend. And maybe he needs to learn a little bit of forgiveness, too. I think he changed his will because of more than just anger toward your mom. I think he just wanted to leave this world knowing you would be able to do what you love without money worries." She took her hand away. "Personally, I think there are more compromises you could make besides the taxes. Compromises that might, in the long run, end up with you and your mom having something between you. Besides anger."

Hannah makes everything sound infuriatingly simple.

I took a deep breath and looked toward the back door just as Miles came out. Mrs. Peterson was in front of him, tottering like a bent-over penguin. She wasn't crying anymore.

My quiet spell was still in effect, so I knew they couldn't hear me ask Hannah, "What in the world is she still doing here? It's been over an hour!" I snapped my fingers and the spell lifted.

"Officer Denton," I said, being formal and professional in front of McCartony and Peterson. And the guy with the tapping toe.

"Ms. Bridges," he answered. "I'll be right with you."

"Ms. Bridges?" Mrs. Peterson said. She looked up through filthy glasses, trying to get a gauge on where my eyes were. "The Ms. Bridges in Esther Sena's building? *The Garden Witch* lady again?"

"Yes, that's me, Mrs. Peterson. You've been in my shop several times. But it's nice to see you again." I reached out and clasped her delicate little hand.

"I've been here talking to this nice policeman about Esther, may she rest in peace," Mrs. Peterson said. Her tongue darted around her dentures, touched her lips, then retreated. "I'd been feeling like I had something to do with her demise, truth be told."

I smiled. The serum behind my ears and the leftovers from my hands might just still be at work.

"I find that hard to believe, Mrs. Peterson," Hannah said warmly. Mrs. Peterson jumped a little at the sound of Hannah's voice, as if she hadn't even noticed she was there.

"I have something for the police to listen to, actually," I said, looking up at Miles. "It might help Mrs. Peterson, too, if you don't mind."

Miles bit the inside of one of his beautiful lips. I could tell he was amused, but at the same time probably wondering what the heck he had gotten himself into, here. He had signed up for big city police work, and here he was, dealing with old people and witches, stolen earrings and bracelets and heart attacks.

"Sure, sure," he said. "Let's all go have a seat and chat." Did he roll his eyes at McCartony as he turned toward the door? I think so.

We sat at the same table where we'd been earlier, and I hit my voice recording button on my phone as soon as we sat down. At the sound of Lloyd Benson's voice, Mrs. Peterson pushed herself back from the table and gave a little gasp that turned into a choking sound. I stopped the recording.

"That snake in the grass!" she said. She covered her eyes with her little hands and rocked herself back and forth on the fold-out chair. I worried she might just fall all the way off.

"He said he loved me! I…I…stayed the night, for heaven's sake! Like a harlot!" She kept her hands up over her face, and I took advantage of the moment to send a little "wow" look to Miles. He gave me the piano key smile.

"And then, then when I realized I'd left my earrings at his apartment, he told me they weren't there. Why, I knew full well they had to be there. I just went over to his place to look for them myself. And that's when he told me that Esther Sena had been wearing my earrings! Imagine, my earrings that her dead husband gave to me when I was just a girl! Why, I've had them for more than half a century! And here she's stealing them away from me just like she stole my Harry!?"

She was crying again. Miles gave me a 'look what you've done' kind of look, then jerked his chin toward my phone. I think he just wanted to get it out and get it done.

I touched the voice recording.

We heard it all from Mr. Benson's mouth, how he'd swapped out her earrings, how he'd done this kind of thing before. It sounded even ickier this time, with his disembodied voice telling this twisted story. My lip was curled even though I really did kind of sympathize with the creepy old guy.

When we got to the part about Lloyd Benson being the "Agent of Change" for all these old ladies, Hannah started the church laughter. At first, she covered with a cough, but then it got down to both of us, holding our noses, me bending over, pretending to be looking through my bag, but really just convulsing in laughter under the table.

Rita Peterson didn't seem to notice, but Miles certainly did. His eyes got wide then squinted. I could tell. He wanted to church laugh, too.

But Officer Miles Denton was a good cop. He settled himself down, heard the Lloyd Benson recording all the way to the end, and let us get our acts together, which we finally did.

"Very helpful, Mad–er, Ms. Bridges. Thank you for your investigative work," he said.

"Oh, sure! Happy to help." I turned to Mrs. Peterson. "Now we know that Hester Diamond, an old girlfriend of Harry Sena's, once had a beautiful bracelet, a simple silver band with little diamonds encrusted along its rims. And when she broke up with him, she gave the bracelet back. And Harry, the old dog, gave it to his next girlfriend, who became his wife. And now, lo and behold, Hester has it back on her wrist. And you," I said, "also dated Harry Sena, and he gave you these."

I carefully unscrewed one earring and let me tell you right here that vintage earrings are for women with very, very high pain thresholds. My earlobes will never be the same.

I placed the earrings gently on the table in front of her.

"They, in turn," I went on, "were 'tucked in' under Phil, the philodendron's pot in Ms. Esther's apartment, the plant I saved but then pushed out a sixth-story window, only to find them in the dirt later on. Mr. Benson had swapped them out for the bracelet that very day."

"We'd had such a quarrel about those earrings right before I stormed out, said Mrs. Peterson. "I know he was angry. But to think! To think he would have the nerve to call the police!

And tell them he'd seen me leave Esther's apartment!" She turned to me and clutched my arm. "As if to imply that I, that I… My goodness. You just can't trust anyone, can you?" Her voice sounded so frail as she finished that I almost cried for her. Then she spat out, "Big dumb jerk!"

We all sat for a second.

"The important thing," said Miles, his voice as smooth as Scotch on a snowy night, "is what I told you earlier tonight. The autopsy report confirms that Esther's heart attack happened just after she went to bed that night, Mrs. Peterson. She was already gone by the time you got there."

Chapter 32: Always be Planting

I heard the tinkle of the little bells on my shop door and wiped my dirty hands on my apron.

"Be right there!" I called, stepping over bags of dirt. "I'm just getting everybody ready for the big spring sale coming up, and I--"

There he was, Officer Miles Denton, standing in my doorway with the sun behind him, a silhouette that dizzied me and dried my mouth. I stopped dead in my tracks.

"Maddie."

"Miles."

"I just came by to check in."

"On me? Or on all the other Perry Street shenanigans?"

"Little bit of both."

"Cup of tea?"

"Please."

I busied myself, frantically fretting over what kind of tea would work best. I mean, *be* best. For Him. I grabbed my trusty green. The caffeine and L-theanine in green or black tea helps in concentration, focus.

I needed him to focus, here.

He made himself at home, wandering through the plants, touching some, smelling others. I kept track of his progress out of the corner of my eye. When the tea was ready and I'd splayed a few shortbread cookies on a plate, he made his way back and sat down. He reached out to touch Phil, who now held a special place smack in the center of my tea table.

"I'm thinking," he started, but then he stopped, cleared his throat, tasted the tea. He blew over it. "I'm thinking maybe, since you've lived here, worked here for years, and I'm still trying to find my way around, that maybe you could help me out."

"Isn't that what I just did?"

The sparkle smile came at me fast and furious.

"Well, yes, professionally speaking. And thank you again for that."

"The autopsy?" I said. "Was that true about the report and the timing?"

"Nah. Well, I guess it could be, but the report was vague on time of death. She just needed to stop blaming herself." He took another sip. "But I'm not here to talk about the case of the missing bracelet."

"Oh, sorry, that's me. Always interrupting. They tell me I have a problem with linear thinking. Whatever that is. I should drink more of this." I laughed. I took a sip of the green, silently telling myself to shut up, shut up, shut up.

His eyes were drilling into me then, and I did. Shut up, I mean.

"I'd like to thank you for that professional help by having you as a guest at my place. I'd like to make dinner for you some night. Soon."

"Ah, the cop turns chef!"

I save the stupid words for important moments. It's what I do.

"Saturday, if you can close a little early?" His eyelashes were curtains of black, and my mind suddenly went to the dream. The dream about him looking through those curtained windows, into the darkness where the skyclad coven waited with candles.

"Maddie?"

"Oh! Oh, well that sounds great, Miles! I'd love that, sure!" I gave him my smile that I practice for selfies in the mirror but was pretty sure it was a goofy rendition of it.

"The dream bags you made?" he said, and my heart just about did an Esther Sena. "Did you have any dreams other than the ones you and Hannah told me about? The troll, which was cute, by the way, and then the one where Mrs. Peterson is walking with Harry Sena. But were there any others?"

"Oh, maybe one or two," I said with a shrug. "I forget to get up and write them all down, though, and they get all jumbly in my head." I didn't want to ruin this whole I'm-going-to-his-house feeling by talking about candlelight and naked witches. But then I had a thought.

"How about you?" I asked. "Did you actually take my bag and sleep on it?" I leaned forward, my mouth just a little bit open in anticipation.

He leaned over the table, over Phil's shiny leaves, just as quick as my favorite rollercoaster the Jack Rabbit, and for one stupid moment I thought he was going to plant a kiss smack on my lips. Everything inside me just went whoosh. But then, just as fast, like if the rollercoaster attendant realized something was wrong and had to shut down the ride, he leaned back into his seat. Just like that.

There was an awkward but charged silence, and thank the gods for Sedona, because she chose that moment to trounce into the room.

"You've got to be kitten me," she said, blinking first at me then at Miles. "What in the–"

"Sedona! I didn't hear you come in. Cream?" I stood up when she nodded, but her eyes were fastened on Miles.

"I have two stories for you," she said. I stopped pouring the cream into her saucer.

"I said *two*," she said.

I poured again until the saucer was almost brimming over.

"What's the first story?" I asked.

She looked up, saw the cream I was holding, and licked her lips. I gave her the stink eye and she sighed.

"Well, Esther spoke to me again. This time in a dream, thanks to your little bag of weeds."

"And?"

"She wants that Hester woman to just keep the silly bracelet. Seems Monday was Hester and Harry's anniversary of their first date. Ha! Esther waits 'til after she's dead to get all philanthropic. Sappy, even." She eyed the saucer again.

"Good one," I said, and Miles and I smiled at each other.

"And the second story?" Miles asked.

"I was just upstairs on two," she said.

"Ah," said Miles. "Scene of the crime. What's new up there?"

"Well, I went up, you know, to collect on the fresh tuna Esther told me, *post mortem,* if you'll remember, that she wanted me to have. Yellowfin, yet. Perfect timing, because her door was open, and it turns out Esther has visitors from Brooklyn. They're up there going through her things, pawing through her drawers and such. Nice women. Apparently both cat lovers.

They couldn't keep their hands off me." She stopped, knowing she had our full attention. "They found the tuna, smelled it and apparently didn't trust it, so they gave it all to me. Ha! Silly women. Didn't even check the date on the wrapper." She took a moment to lick her front right paw. Then she used it to clean behind her right ear.

"Sedona!" I said. "Spill! Who are they?"

She looked up and licked her lips.

"Cream please!" she said.

"Not until you spill." At this, I actually did spill a bit of cream. Sedona's eye shot down to the floor and before I knew it she was lapping up the drops. I clenched my teeth.

"I'm not sure you're going to like my spill, Maddie," she finally said when all the drops of cream were gone.

Miles and I looked at each other, then back at her.

"Seems they found Esther Sena's will in her underwear drawer," Sedona went on. "They were pleased with most of it, and if I was hearing correctly, they're the granddaughters. Esther skipped right over her own children and left most of her money and belongings to them."

"Well, I guess that's her prerogative," I said, thinking of my dad. "Maybe I should go up and introduce myself."

"That's exactly what I would suggest," said Sedona. "Because there was another person named in the will. The person who has been left a significant portion of Esther Sena's estate. This building, in fact." Sedona stopped staring at the cream in my hand and smiled at me.

"It's funny, really," she said, her tail flicking. "They're shaking their heads over the will and one says to the other, 'Who in the world is Madeline Brooklyn Bridges?'"

About the Author

Laurie Holding lives with her husband in Sewickley, Pennsylvania, a village not at all like Greenwich Village. She is the author of two children's books, *Tyrion's Tale* and *Tyrion's Town,* about her dog Tyrion, who is a survivor of a dogfighting ring. She is a fiction author working under various pen names in collaboration with other writers of science fiction, mystery, thrillers, and short stories.

An award-winning poet, Laurie's work has placed or won in the Goodreads Poetry Forum, Writer's Digest Annual Poetry Contest, and the Maria W. Faust Sonnet Contest. Her first poetry chapbook is scheduled for a 2021 release.

Planted on Perry Street is her first solo novel. All Garden Witch Cozy Mysteries will appear under the pen name L. B. Holding.

You can connect with me on:

https://www.laurieholding.com

https://www.facebook.com/authorlbholding

Made in the USA
Middletown, DE
12 March 2021

35431960R00117